THE LYON RESISTANCE

RICHARD WAKE

PART I

1

The small railroad bridge, our target for the night, was about halfway between Lyon and Saint Etienne, maybe 10 miles from each, give or take. The tracks ran close to the Rhone on one side and were hugged by farmland on the other. The land was relatively flat there, and simple grade crossings over the roadways were sufficient — except in this one place, where a dip in the land called for a little stone bridge to hold the tracks over an unnamed road dividing fields of hay. Although, on my scouting trips, it never seemed that big of a dip. This might have been one of those fortuitous occasions where a local elected official owned both the land that the railroad company needed and the little stone bridge construction company.

Railroad track demolition was one of the ways we annoyed the Germans. We had to admit, though, that it was mostly just that: an annoyance. If you blew up a few yards of tracks on a Wednesday night, you would screw up traffic in and out of Lyon on Thursday. If you were lucky, on Friday, too. But that was it — and it seemed that the Nazis were getting better at the business of repairing the blown lines. They also were bringing in an increasing number of men to perform regular preventative patrols.

So it was getting to be a lose-lose calculation — unless you were talking about a bridge. Because the destruction of even the smallest bridge, like the single stone arch I was looking at through my binoculars as I lay behind a hay bale, would put the line out of business for at least a week, and more likely two. The risk-reward suddenly tilted again toward reward, even while acknowledging that the German did the same cost-benefit analysis and kept a close eye on every bridge along the line, including the tiny ones. Which was why Rene, Max and I kept trading the glasses between us, staring at the back of the heads of the two German soldiers leaning on the fenders of their vehicle. They were smoking cigarettes. When they turned, you could see the tiny glow.

"How much time?" Max said. Rene looked at his watch.

"Still five minutes," he said. "No, six. Relax."

Max scooted away from us, crab-walking behind another hay bale to take a piss. If they gave tests to spies, or saboteurs, or resistance agents, or whatever the fuck we were, the adequate bladder test would have flunked Max out straight away. He was a good kid, only 17 and entirely cold-blooded — he very nearly severed the head of a German sentry he had already killed, just in a rage, during a mission to set a fuel depot on fire. But he had to piss as often as an old man, which was the only thing I could kid him about, seeing as how I was 42 years old and he called me Pops. As in, "Fuck you, Pops," which was essentially his reply to everything I said.

If I was the brains of the operation — and in all modesty, I was — and if Max supplied the muscle and the balls, Rene was the demolitions expert. How he had acquired the expertise had never been explained to me, but Rene knew about the different types of explosives, and how to attach the detonator and the wires and, in this case, the windup alarm clock. I had been given a quick-and-dirty training session once, and I could wire an explosive charge to a plunger, but I would never trust myself with one of the timers. You have to know your limits, especially when you are talking about dismemberment.

Max had argued about everything when we set up the first charge, at about 10 p.m. It was on the tracks, maybe 300 yards from the little stone bridge.

"Pops, we're too fucking close," he said.

"We have to be close," I said. Then I explained to him for the fifth time that in order for this to work, the soldiers guarding the bridge had to be close enough to the first explosion that they felt it was their clear and obvious duty to investigate it themselves.

"But we need the time," Max said. "They could reach us with their rifles if they saw us."

"They're not going to see us," I said. "They're going to be running toward the explosion, and then they're going to be staring at burning railroad ties and radioing back to whoever for instructions. As soon as they start heading for the explosion, we start heading for the bridge. We'll get where we need to be before they get to the explosion. And how much time do you need, Rene?"

"Two minutes, Alex," he said. "It's all packed in the cases. I just need to set the timers. Maybe less than two minutes once I'm on the bridge. The cases are pretty heavy for me to carry up that embankment, though."

"That's what Max is for," I said.

"Fuck you, Pops."

And so it went. We set the timer on the first charge to go off at 11 p.m. We still had three minutes. Now I had to piss. I could have held it, but I felt as if maybe Max needed to win one before the end of the night. So I crab-walked behind the same bale and listened to him mock me.

"Mine's just nerves, and I can always learn to relax," he said. "But your old man plumbing is shot forever."

As this went on, Rene continued to stare at his watch. He gave a one-minute warning, then 30 seconds. The three of us were ready to move when the explosion went off, piercing the night. I watched through the binoculars as the two soldiers jumped, then said something to each other, then hesitated, then began running toward the boom and what was now a fire of burning railroad ties. One of them was carrying a portable radio and holding it up to his ear as he ran. The other held his helmet down with one hand and grabbed his rifle with the other.

"All right, let's do it," I said. We all trotted, Max carrying the suitcases full of dynamite, Rene and I with pistols drawn. From there, it went pretty much exactly as I had planned it out in my head. The embankment was not that steep, pretty easy for all of us, even Max with the cases. On my scouting trips — which were necessarily brief, to avoid suspicion — I had noticed that there was a space on each side of the bridge, between the railroad bed and the keystone of each arch. I was pretty confident that Rene would be able to wedge the cases into the space, but you don't know until you know.

"They going to fit?" I said.

"Like a glove, Alex my boy. Like a fucking glove."

I don't think he took 90 seconds to get the clocks set and put the cases in place. The entire time, I could see the two soldiers, outlined against the fire on the tracks. We ran past our original vantage point to another, maybe 400 yards away. As we got set, Rene looked at his watch.

"Two minutes," he said, and then pointed to the binoculars. "May I?"

"Yes, the artist should see his masterpiece," I said.

We all stood now, not even hiding. It was a moonless night, chosen for that very reason, and cloudy besides. Nobody was looking at us. I took one more quick peek toward the first explosion and saw the same two silhouettes. Then I focused back on the little stone bridge, just in time to see it reduced to a little stone pile. The two explosions came about 10 seconds apart.

As Rene stared into the binoculars — "Ah, it's beautiful," he said, once, then twice — Max and I instinctively hugged each other as if we had just assisted on a game-winning goal during stoppage time. But then we had to go, three men dressed like farm laborers to three different farms in the area. From there, we would be transported back to Lyon.

"You both memorized your directions, right?" I said. "And stay off the roads."

"Fuck you, Pops," Max said.

2

My farm was in Chassagny. Our plan was to sleep rough in the fields behind the three farms where we were headed, the assumption being that the Gestapo would be knocking on doors before dawn in their search for the bridge saboteurs. I didn't think I would be able to sleep, but I did, the adrenaline rush long past and leaving only exhaustion in its place. It was the rising sun that woke me, and then the slamming of the back door of the farmhouse in the distance as Marcel Lefebvre headed to the barn and his cows. I followed him in, a minute or two later, and I startled him. He fell off of his milking stool and came within inches of compounding the indignity by landing in a pile of cow shit.

"You missed them," he said. He was on his feet now and embracing me.

"Missed who?"

"Your friends in the black leather coats," he said. "They were banging on the door at 3:30. They searched the house and the barn with torches and warned me to be on the lookout for some Resistance saboteurs."

"They're just paranoid," I said.

"I hope they have something to be paranoid about," Marcel said.

I told him about the little stone bridge, and he dropped a teat to thrust his hand toward the sky. Then he continued milking. I watched in silence as he filled a pail. It didn't take long.

"Everybody's okay, right?" he said. When I assured him we were, he motioned for me to follow him into the house. "Quick, quick, just in case," he said, and we scampered inside.

From a barrel in the corner of the kitchen, he poured us two tumblers of rough red wine. I looked at my watch theatrically. It was 7:15 a.m.

"Hell, we're celebrating," Marcel said, shoving the glass at me.

"I wasn't complaining," I said.

"You'd better not be — this is a good batch."

Marcel was in his fifties, a widower with no kids — which meant he did everything on his little hay farm, including delivering the hay to his customers. That is how I would be returning to Lyon, secreted in his hay wagon. For fun, and for some extra money, he made wine. There were some real wineries nearby, but his was a grapes-in-the-bathtub-sized operation. He sold mostly to friends, or at local farmers' markets. He had some beautiful old oak barrels, and the wine he made was significantly better than crap, an everyday wine that was noticeably tastier than typical everyday wine. Of course, given the rationing, even crap wine was very much in demand.

He worked hard at it, as a kind of profitable hobby, and had about 25 barrels in the barn. As it turned out, those barrels were why he joined the Resistance. With petrol in low supply and a lot of car motors converted to burning wood, the Germans did a different kind of conversion. They had engines that would run on alcohol, that would run on wine. And so, they traveled the countryside and went about the business of requisitioning all the wine they could get their hands on.

"It's bad enough they wouldn't pay for it," Marcel said, when he first told me the story. "But Alex, I could live with that. I understand pigs. But when they dumped motor oil in with the wine, I just couldn't take that."

The problem wasn't that the oil spoiled the wine for drinking because it did. That was the Germans' purpose. The issue was the barrels. The oil ruined them, too, leaving behind a residue that soaked into the old wood and could not be cleaned out. They couldn't be used for wine anymore.

"I cried when I had to break them up," Marcel said. He used them for firewood.

"How many did they get?"

"Twelve."

"How many did you manage to hide from them?"

"Fourteen," he said. Then he laughed. "With these assholes, the way I figure it, I'm still ahead of the game, 14-12. And now, I help you guys out here and there, and the wine I have left tastes that much sweeter."

He pulled two empty bottles out of the cupboard, filled one with wine and one with milk, and stoppered them. "Here," he said, handing them over. "We need to get going."

With that, my bottles and I climbed into the wagon. He had square bales already loaded — three layers of bales, five in a row, five deep, 75 bales in all. Except it was really 73, as I found out when I crawled into an empty space in the middle of the hay structure and then sat as Marcel sealed me in.

He had asked me ahead of time if it was necessary, and I admitted that this was exercising an insane level of caution. I mean, it wasn't as if every other wagon headed into town with farm goods was manned by a single person.

"So you're my helper — what's the big deal?" Marcel said.

"You're probably right," I said. "But what if you get stopped by a German who knows you live alone here, and work alone? I'm sure they're really on edge, really jumpy, and it's just not worth the risk, even if you just told them I was a day laborer helping with a big load."

So I sat in darkness, save for a tiny shaft of light — and, presumably, oxygen — that made it through the immense pile. And, as it turned out, Marcel was stopped by a German patrol, and one of the soldiers did jab a bayonet into the hay bales two or three times for show. If the steel had struck flesh, it would have been a lot harder for Marcel to explain than a strange day laborer sitting next to him in the passenger seat. But the bayonet hit nothing besides hay, and we made it to the Lyon municipal stables by 10 o'clock. Yes, I was being smuggled into the place where the city police boarded their horses.

"Don't worry," Marcel said. The wagon was parked behind the barns. No one was around. "Besides," he said, "now you can be my day laborer."

"It's worth it for the wine and the milk," I said. We had the truck unloaded within an hour. Then, Marcel made sure to pull every stray bit of hay out of my hair and pockets and cuffs. If I walked fast, I would be home in another hour.

3

The walk home took me past the old army medical school, which was now Gestapo headquarters in Lyon — just one more bit of evidence of God's twisted sense of humor. What once had been a place where men were taught to save the lives of those who had been thrust into hell was now a place where the hell was manufactured instead.

The Gestapo had been in Lyon for four months. We were all in church when they arrived — literally. It was November 11, 1942, and we were praying for the dead of the first war on the anniversary of the armistice. And if everyone in the church was praying for the French war dead, and I was praying for the friends I lost while fighting for Austria-Hungary, so be it. We were on the same side now. When we walked out of the church together, the German columns were arriving. We were in the free zone for the first two years of the war, the part of France the Germans couldn't be bothered with and left to the fucking Vichy to run things. But then, seemingly overnight, we were worthy of their attention. The brass piled into the Hotel Terminus, across from the train station, and attempted to operate from there for a while. But the business of torture and terror, a booming industry, quickly outgrew the hotel's accommodations. So while they continued to use the Terminus as their dormitory, the Gestapo had taken over the old medical school on Avenue Berthelot, a block and a half from the Rhone, for their hijinks.

I could have avoided it, but I liked walking by — big and solid, Nazi flags flying, black-uniformed sentries at the gate. It reminded me why I was doing this. I made Manon walk by with me the last time we were close. And while she didn't object, she did say, "You know full well that I don't need a fucking reminder."

Manon was my wife. We met in Zurich in late 1939. I followed her to Lyon, her home, after the German invasion in 1940. We had fallen in love despite a rather unconventional romantic beginning — unconventional in the sense that she was a spy for the French intelligence service who seduced me because she was trying to figure out what I was up to, me being a spy for the former Czech government in exile and all. As it turned out, we possessed not only a physical and an emotional attraction, but we also bonded over a professional realization that became clear as the panzers sped through the Ardennes: we worked for idiots, for blind men married to the past, for cowards incapable of action.

So now we worked for the Resistance, and for each other, and against the black uniforms and the swastika flags. We published an underground newspaper, one of a half-dozen in the city, called *La Dure Vérité*. It was really a sheet or two run off on a Roneo machine, once or twice a month, but we were convinced it made a difference, maybe even more than the sabotage — railroad tracks, telephone lines, whatever would disrupt the German terror machine. We were sure that the 1,000 copies we produced were being read by 20,000, passed secretly from hand to hand. Of course, there were also days when we were convinced that nobody was reading anything and that nothing mattered. Those were the days I went out of my way to walk down Avenue Berthelot, to watch the red flags starched in the breeze, to see the sharpness in the creases in the black SS uniforms. And, maybe to see Barbie.

Klaus Barbie was the man in charge and I had never seen him. There already were stories of his brutality, but how much was true and how much was an urban legend was unclear. It seemed as if everybody's horrible story was third-hand. If he really was torturing and killing people, and doing it personally, they wouldn't be around to tell the tales, after all. I didn't know anybody who had been in his presence for more than a few seconds.

Max had seen Barbie on the street, arriving at Avenue Berthelot one day, and said, "He's fucking short. He's not one of those big, tall, blond assholes." He guessed Barbie was maybe five-foot-six. Another friend had heard his voice once, outside the Terminus as he was waiting for a car. "He speaks French — he was talking to the valet at the front door, and he was doing okay with the language. Just really slow."

But as for the rest, the rumors of torture and brutality, they were just that. Still, I was dying to put a face to a name, maybe just to give myself a more vivid nightmare. On this day, though, as on all the others when I walked by, I didn't see him. And now that I thought about it, maybe that was what made the nightmares worse.

I crossed the Rhone and then walked north, up to our neighborhood, the Croix-Rousse, up the steep hills, so steep that sometimes there was a stone staircase to take you up from one cross street to the next. Our house, a tiny single with a tinier patch of grass out front, was a few blocks away from Manon's family business, a silk manufacturing factory that her uncle ran by himself since her father's death a few years back. Manon helped with the bookkeeping and used a storeroom in the back as the base of our underground publishing empire. Our Resistance cell was tiny — Manon and I, and a couple of others — and we met in the factory when it was necessary. Which meant twice in the last year, and one of those times was just an excuse to get drunk together after I came into possession of a case of bootleg wine. The other time was to tell them that the various Resistance groups had been forced to come together into a kind of confederation after Barbie and his pals arrived, and that our sabotage work would have to be coordinated. That's how I ended up working with Rene and Max, who were with Combat and Liberation, much bigger Resistance groups than ours.

As I approached the house, Manon was sitting on the little front porch, taking a bit of the afternoon sun. Eyes closed, face upturned — God, she was beautiful. She greeted me in the time-honored fashion, and after we were done, we lay naked in the bed and she whispered softly, "Enough of this. I'd kill for a glass of that milk. And then a glass of the wine."

I feigned annoyance. She reached down and grabbed me there. "The milk and the wine are rationed," she said. "This isn't. Not yet, anyway."

We pulled on robes and sat at the kitchen table and drank first from the milk bottle and then from the wine bottle, just passing them back and forth, not even using glasses. I recounted what I had been doing the last two days, and Manon kissed me on the forehead and called me her "little mad bomber." She told me a funny story about her uncle and the half-deaf old woman who ran one of the looms, screaming at each other about a botched order. The sun felt warm through the front window. Winter was done now.

Both bottles were about half-empty, maybe a little more, when the knock on the door signaled the arrival of three Gestapo men, two of them with guns drawn. One of them came into our bedroom and watched me get dressed, and then it was into the backseat.

4

It was well into the afternoon, and apparently the Gestapo worked bankers' hours, so they didn't take me to Avenue Berthelot. Instead, after escorting me to the car, and with Manon watching stoically from the porch, they drove me to Montluc Prison.

"PRISON MILITAIRE," is what the sign said over the main gate, and that it was — an old shithole built originally to house the military's criminal problems, mostly prisoners of war from the last time. By 1943, though, it had become the Gestapo's holding pen for the people it wanted to hold and an execution site for those who no longer held the jailers' fancy. The guards were French, but the orders handed down were quite German. To come here was not to receive a death sentence, not necessarily, but the cells weren't filled with drunks and wife beaters and petty thieves, either. The Germans didn't care so much about crimes committed against people unless they were German people. Montluc was a place for dealing with crimes against the Nazi vision. Oh, and for dealing with Jews.

I didn't resist when I was arrested, mostly because if I had, Manon might have jumped to my assistance and gotten herself hauled in, too. Also, there were the guns to consider. I always considered the guns. During the ride over, I stuck to speaking French to the Gestapo gorillas, not wanting to alert them to the fact that I spoke German. Then I tried to eavesdrop on their chatter as if it would provide me with some morsel I might use to escape. Instead, all I found out was the name of the bar they were going to drink in after work. Jenney's.

After we walked through the gate, my escorts could not wait to be rid of me. They skipped out of the prison as if freed from a 10-year stretch, which strongly suggested there might be a during-work stop somewhere else, before Jenney's. I was left to sit on a bench in a holding cell, waiting for someone to fill out my paperwork. A fat, half-untucked French guard eventually came for me and checked me in.

"Name?"

"Allain Killy," I said.

"Papers?"

I handed them over. My real name was Alex Kovacs, which was duly recorded in my Czech, Austrian and Swiss passports; it's a long story. For my first year in Lyon, I went by Alex. In 1941, I was convinced for operational reasons by other Resistance members to create a second identity. That's when I became Albert Kampe. In 1942, I added Allain Killy. My friends, and most people in the Resistance, still called me Alex. Some called me Al, others AK. The point was to have several valid sets of identity papers so that, if I were arrested, I could change identities. That way, if I were arrested a second time, only the memory of a policeman or Gestapo agent would link me to the previous arrest. The name itself wouldn't set off any alarm bells if somebody saw it on a list.

Which meant that the identity would have to be retired. It was going to be au revoir, Allain, once I got out of Montluc. Which was maybe a fantasy, I knew.

"Belt," said the untucked concierge, and I handed it over.

"Shoelaces," he said, and I handed them over, too.

"Get naked," he said. He searched my clothes as I stood there, hands instinctively covering my privates. He ran his hands carefully over all of the seams of the pants and shirt, and the hems of my cuffs. He eyed up the soles of my shoes and then banged them together as if hoping to feel the vibration of a weapon secreted somewhere inside. He skipped over the peek up my butthole, likely for his benefit more than mine. Then, apparently satisfied, or maybe just bored, or both, he handed everything back.

"Get dressed," he said, and turned and left me to it. But any hope I had that this was just going to be a courtesy visit, just taking down my name and warning me about something or other, was tempered by the knowledge that they had already taken my belt and shoelaces. And in a minute — I just had time to get buttoned up — another guard arrived to escort me out of the intake building, across a courtyard of sorts, and then into the building that housed the cells.

It was two floors of cells. Each floor had about 24 cells, 12 on each side. On the second floor, there was a balcony effect, with the cells along the perimeter and an open area between them, a railing separating you from the view of the first floor below. There was metal fencing that prevented anyone falling from the second floor down to the tile on the first floor. Or, more likely, jumping.

My accommodations were on the second floor. Each cell was maybe 6 feet wide and 12 feet deep. The walls were painted dark gray on the bottom half and white above that to the ceiling. The floors were dark tile of some sort. There were two straw mattresses on each floor, and there was a stinking bucket in the far right corner. My cell contained four prisoners — I was the fourth, when they slammed the heavy wooden door behind me — and that seemed about the norm. I didn't recognize anybody.

There was not much conversation among the four of us beyond an initial hello. Honestly, no one knew who might be a Gestapo informant, so there was no way we could even consider trusting each other at the outset. It was impossible for me to tell them, "I blew up a train bridge, and how about you?" So there was just silence, and some outward courtesies as we took turns laying down on the two straw mattresses. That they were undoubtedly infested with lice didn't matter, either to them or to me.

Really, the only thing anyone said after the initial greeting was when the one guy, an older guy, even older than me, stood up from the mattress, muttered "my apologies in advance," and proceeded to take the nosiest shit I can remember in the open bucket in the corner. It almost would have been comical if it had not been so dehumanizing. And the smell, well, it was constant after that.

"When do they empty it?" I said.

"Tomorrow." It was the youngest guy in the group. I'm not sure he was 17. I wondered if his parents knew where he was. I was going crazy, and attempted some conversation with him, as benign a conversation as I could conjure.

"How long have you been here?" He was wary, but then he answered.

"Three days, I think," he said.

"Been outside of here in that time?"

"No, other than to wash my face. There's a sink down at the end of the hall with four spigots. We get one wash a day. Oh, and a quick walk around the courtyard."

"Food?"

"Stale bread and cold coffee in the morning — the fake coffee." This was the fourth guy, 30-ish, almost bald. "Cold stew at night, no meat. That should be coming soon. It's shit, but you have to eat something."

He also had been in the cell for three days. The old guy said he was on his fifth day. The food arrived, and we stopped talking. It was shoved through a panel in the thick wood door, and it was as advertised — shit. Soon after we ate, it was dark and so quiet, at least for a few minutes. The four of us arranged ourselves so that each of us at least had our head on the mattress. As I settled down, it wasn't the smell that bothered me the most, or the lice that I knew were crawling on me. It was the cloud of flies, which gathered during the day near the top of the tall cells, up near the light. Because when the light went out, the flies would dive-bomb from on high, and you would attempt to sleep between swats and whispered curses.

5

I knew nothing about the inside of Montluc before I arrived, but I did know that there was a procedure for finding out if someone you knew was being held there. You showed up with some clothing or food and said this was for so-and-so. If the package was accepted that meant so-and-so was there. And so I was greeted in the morning by a guard bearing a small package, wrapped in brown paper, that had apparently been opened and re-wrapped by the guards. Manon had come to find me. Inside was a shirt, underwear, socks, and four apples. And so my new roommates and I had an addition to our breakfast menu of fake coffee and stale bread.

I looked around the room, just to make sure I hadn't missed it, and I hadn't. None of the other three had any belongings other than what they were wearing, which meant that their families did not know where they were. Or maybe they had no loved ones in the area. Whatever, it was hard for me to reconcile how filled with love and support I felt at that moment, and compare it to the face of the young kid in the cell as he sat in the corner and gnawed on the apple, spitting out a few of the seeds but eating every other bit of it except for the stem. He was crying as he ate it, but his face was still hard as he wiped a tear with his dirty sleeve.

After we ate, we were permitted a quick walk around the courtyard, maybe 10 minutes' worth. It was not an organized exercise period. We walked in a great circle around the perimeter of the yard, guards with rifles keeping us moving and in line as we snaked around the facility. I thought I saw Max about 100 people ahead of me, but I wasn't sure and couldn't maneuver out of the line to get a view of anything other than the backs of a few heads. Max. Fuck. I wondered if they got Rene, too – and then I was pretty sure I saw him, too, way off in the distance. But how? Had one of them been caught at their farm house? Had they talked?

At one point, we entered a part of the yard that featured a low building that had apparently been added recently. It butted up against the taller jail. There was still the smell of freshly cut lumber in the air, and scatterings of sawdust. It seemed as if there was an original structure, and that they were adding to it.

I poked the kid from my cell and pointed.

"What's that?"

"Jews," he said.

"What?"

"That's where they put the Jews."

We continued walking. We got close enough that, when a door of these new barracks opened, I could see inside for a second. There were rows of bunks, one on top of another on top of another. But it was just a peek as the door slammed shut.

After our exercise, all of the prisoners were led back inside and told to wait outside of our cells. It was crowded, like a train platform at rush hour, except more haggard. The hopelessness on so many of the faces forced me to stare down at my shoes. In a minute, a guard with a clipboard began reading names. It was a list of 20 altogether. They were divided into two groups.

"With luggage," the guard bellowed. "With luggage." And then he called off 10 names, last name then first name.

"Now," the guard said, yelling even louder. "Without luggage. I repeat: without luggage." And then he read 10 more names. Heads noticeably fell as these names were read. There was the occasional gasp. One such gasp came from just to my right. It came from the old man in our cell, the one who had taken the noisy shit. Jean Bisset was his name.

"All names I have just read will report to me, either with or without your luggage," the guard said. "You have two minutes. Now everyone back into your cells."

The four of us were back inside, and the three of us not named Jean Bisset were leaning against different walls. I don't know if we were trying to give him some space or to give ourselves some distance. Two minutes of silence can be forever sometimes, and this was. We didn't look him in the eye but it didn't matter because Bisset's face was covered by his hands. He wasn't crying, but it was as if he couldn't bear to look, either. And then, whatever emotion had gripped him appeared to pass. His hands came down from his face and his look was nothing short of defiant.

"If they call your name..." he said. And then he stopped as his voice caught. And then he started again.

"If anyone ever asks," he said, "tell them that Jean Bisset's final moments were brave moments. Vive la France."

And then, just as he reached the cell door, he turned and looked at me, smiled and winked, and said, "And thanks for the apple."

That's when I started crying, just after he left. I sat in the corner of that filthy shithole and blubbered. It took me a few minutes to look up and ask, "With luggage? Without luggage?"

The bald guy answered. "With luggage means you are being

transferred somewhere else, likely to some kind of camp," he said. "And without luggage..."

He stopped. Within seconds, the silence was pierced by rifle fire. Without luggage meant death. Everybody knew what was happening, and how the risks of resisting the Germans were both real and enormous, but the series of percussive blasts provided an awful affirmation for me, or punctuation. For a while, I could hardly catch my breath.

Then keys jangled in the hallway and the enormous wooden door swung open. The wood must have been close to four inches thick. The hinges strained and groaned at each opening.

"Killy, Allain," the guard said, and I stood up. "It's your lucky day. You are going for a ride on the Avenue Berthelot Express. Come."

He walked me out where I joined five others. I looked at the clock on the wall and it was 9 o'clock exactly. We were loaded onto the back of an open lorry and cuffed, both hands, to manacles that were secured to the floor with heavy iron chains. The slatted walls were high enough to shield us from the wind and the eyes of people on the streets, but the open top afforded us the ability to follow the route. The guard and driver were both French, not Gestapo. None of us in the back said a word.

It was an odd route. We came out of the back of the prison and down a couple of side streets as if there was an intention to avoid the busier roads. I wasn't an expert on the neighborhood, but it seemed to me that Rue Garibaldi made the most sense for the heart of the trip, which probably wasn't even two miles long. But we took lefts and right on little streets and even went through some kind of army facility. I thought I saw a sign that said "Fort La Motte," but I wasn't sure of anything, except that I had never heard of it. Whatever, it seemed a rather indirect route, rather inefficient, more French than German.

When we arrived at Avenue Berthelot, a gate was opened and we were driven into a vast central courtyard. My first thought was that it was far enough away from the street that only a dedicated gawker could see what was going on inside — and, well, let's just say that the black-clad sentries were not big fans of dedicated gawkers. There were buildings on three sides of the courtyard, with the gate and stone walls along the street forming the fourth side. The buildings were four stories tall, made of a grayish-brown stone. A flagpole was the only interruption in the vast expanse of the courtyard. A giant red Nazi flag riffled in a significant breeze. The bits of brass hardware that held the flag to the lines were clanking against the white metal pole.

We sat in the lorry for about five minutes before two Gestapo soldiers arrived to unshackle us — or, rather, to order the French guards to unshackle us. They treated the French guards like shit — "Hurry up, you're all the fucking same," said one, in German — with a lack of courtesy that bordered on disdain. I could only imagine what was next for me.

I found out in just a few seconds when one guard pulled a list out of his breast pocket and said, "Killy, Allain?"

I stepped forward.

"It's your lucky day, Killy, Allain. The rest go to the basement. You get to meet our Commander Barbie."

6

The office was on the fourth floor. I was escorted to the door by the guard and left there with a soldier sitting at a desk outside. Other than that I was wearing pants that had to be held up by my hand and shoes without shoelaces, and that I had taken my last shit in a bucket in a fly-infested cell in front of three strangers, I might have been a salesman waiting on an appointment with the boss of the factory. Which I was in a previous life. It was about five years earlier, but it seemed like 50.

Sitting there, I tried to decide on a story to tell. I had been so freaked out by my experience in the cell that I hadn't been able to concentrate, but as I watched the junior Hitler sitting at the desk next to me, filling out forms and then getting up and dropping them into a filing cabinet, it was clearly now or never.

The problem was that I had no idea what they knew. There was no way, no way in hell, that they had seen us blow up the little stone bridge. There were no witnesses. It wasn't as if somebody took our picture in the dark. We had all arrived at the site, on separate trains, at stations miles apart, at different times. There was no way, and the only thing to do was deny everything. And that was true even if either Max or Rene had given up my name. They were going to do with me whatever they were going to do. That was not in my control. I felt like throwing up, but I had known this day was always a possibility. The only thing I controlled was my story. And I wasn't there. I was home with Manon. Fin.

I repeated this over and over as if it were a mantra. I might have been doing that for a half-hour before Barbie showed up.

He was, indeed, short. Max had been right — five-foot-six, maybe. There was nothing particularly menacing about his physical appearance, other than the black uniform, which always tightened my sphincter — undoubtedly the point. But the man himself seemed harmless just to look at, ordinary, neither handsome nor ugly. Just a guy.

Except for the dog — a German shepherd, naturally — that strained at its leash and bared its teeth and growled as it approached me.

"Hildy, Hildy," Barbie said, and the dog immediately backed down. He looked at me. "I'm sorry, Monsieur Killy. She means no harm. Please, please, follow me in."

Barbie and the dog went first through the door, and I did as instructed. The office was huge, clearly the office of someone in charge. Perhaps at one time it was the school's chief medical officer. Now, it was this, this Barbie.

"Sit, sit," he said, pointing at the chair next to his desk. There was another chair that was directly across from the desk and would have created more of a power dynamic for him, but he chose the side chair for me instead, the one his secretary likely sat in when he took dictation or summarized some report or other. Hildy crawled up on a small rug behind the desk, seeming to relax but never taking her eyes off me. After a few seconds, I was so spooked that I couldn't even look at her.

We sat in silence as Barbie toyed with some paperwork on his desk. Whether it was a file on me, or a report of the blown up bridge, I didn't know. He seemed barely interested in it, riffling through the last few pages, barely scanning what was written. Maybe it was a file about something else entirely. But if he was trying to make me even more nervous with the delay, he was succeeding splendidly. I could feel my hands shaking as they sat in my lap.

Finally, he ended the silence.

"So, Monsieur Killy, you are probably wondering what has brought you to the attention of the Gestapo today. Yes?"

His French was, indeed, as advertised: good but slow. He pronounced the words precisely and accurately. The idiom was a bit stiff, as if from a textbook. But after a few more basic questions and answers — my age, address, marital status, occupation — Barbie stopped and asked, "Your accent? Where are you from?"

So he had a good ear. My accent was Alsatian because, growing up in Czechoslovakia, the family cook who taught me French was from Alsace. So that, combined with an adulthood speaking German while I lived in Vienna, accounted for the accent. Except that Barbie and I weren't quite friendly enough for me to tell him the story of my upbringing and my professional life, including when I was spying against the Germans for the Czech government. Perhaps another time.

"You have a good ear," I said. "I grew up in Brumath, near Strasbourg." It was a place I had chosen from a map. It was one of the smaller dots on the map of Alsace that I could find.

"I try to hear the accents," he said, and smiled. He apparently was proud of himself. The smile lasted about two seconds. Then Barbie picked up the file folder, opened it, and began reading.

"Late on Tuesday night, a railroad bridge was blown up by saboteurs near the town of Mornant. What do you know about that?"

"Nothing," I said. I'm sure my voice betrayed my fear. My guess is that Barbie would have been disappointed if it hadn't.

"There were actually two explosions," he said. "Very clever — one as a diversion for the soldiers guarding the bridge, the second for the bridge itself. Very clever. Very tactically sound."

He looked at me as if he were seeking a response. I just stared back and waited for him to continue, which he did.

"Where were you on Tuesday night?"

"At home with my wife."

"Can you prove that?"

"Prove? No. But you can ask her." This was the standard alibi that Manon and I, and every Resistance husband and wife, had worked out.

"We have. Or we will."

I didn't think they'd brought her in, or hurt her — after all, she had been at the prison in the morning with my package. But it gave me something else to worry about other than myself, which was actually a relief.

I sat in silence for another 30 seconds as Barbie set the file down, open, and turned its pages, one by one. He was paying more attention this time through, or at least it appeared he was. Finally, he looked up.

"That is all, Monsieur Killy," he said. "You may go."

He did not stand, or shake my hand, or see me out. He went back to his file. I stood, and Hildy perked up for a second, showing just a hint of her teeth. But as I retreated to the door, she did not growl or follow. As I opened the door to leave, I looked back for one last peek. The dog's head was on the little rug and Barbie was concentrating on the file more closely, his finger tracing across one of the lines as he read.

7

W e stood there, five of us, waiting in the courtyard for the next express bus back to Montluc. But my companions were different than the passengers with whom I had arrived, at least to the best of my memory. Perhaps they ran more than one shuttle per day.

I didn't stare, seeing as how it seemed rude and the last thing any of us needed was more shit to deal with, but my four new friends all looked like hell. It was only after we were in the back of the lorry, manacled to the floor, that I got a better look at everyone. And it made me feel all the more unsettled.

One guy was wet, as if he had been bathed while wearing his clothes. He was shivering, and as pale as I had ever seen a human being. As for the other three, two of them were missing fingers that I was pretty sure had been attached when they woke up that morning. The one guy to my left was missing the pinky on his left hand. The poor bastard next to him was missing his left pinky and ring finger, which suggested a bit of over-exuberance on the part of the craftsman wielding the nippers or a bit of over-recalcitrance from the poor bastard. Or maybe both. Whatever — the hands were not even bandaged. They had stopped bleeding, but the stumps were still raw and disgusting.

Then there was the fourth guy, who looked almost as pale as the soaked guy but otherwise unharmed. There was, however, a telltale: blood had soaked through from the inside of his right shoe and had begun to ooze over the ridge between the upper and the sole. If I had to guess, he was at least a pinky toe lighter, and perhaps more.

I felt embarrassed to be sitting there, still intact. I felt like itching theatrically to show them that the lice had gotten to my right arm. I felt like screaming, "Hey, I had to shit in a bucket last night, too."

But the question still screamed back:

Why had Barbie just let me go?

Maybe that was just how it worked. Maybe they built up to the really bad stuff, growing the tension as in a horror movie. Quiet, creepy talk the first day, then the nippers the second day, then, well, I had no idea. Whenever I was on this topic, my mind invariably ended up at my worst fear: electrodes attached to a car battery on one end and my balls on the other. I once confessed this fear to Manon, and she laughed.

"I wonder what Dr. Freud would say about that," she said.

"Other than that I have a healthy fear of getting my balls electrocuted, like every sentient male, I don't think there is anything to say."

But if this was all a Gestapo tactic, ratcheting up the tension, I just didn't know. And it wasn't as if I could ask. We were all still in a position of not knowing who might or might not be a Gestapo agent in shitty clothing. Besides, they all appeared to be shaken beyond the capability of polite conversation.

We took the same odd route back to the prison. Part of me figured it was just the guards extending their time outside of the prison walls and away from their bosses. But it was the exact same route, just in reverse, every left now a right, every right now a left. The guards were French, not German, so they weren't genetically married to a list of instructions. They could have gone a different way. They could have taken even a slower, more circuitous route, if delay was the purpose. But, no. This was a precise plan, rights as lefts now, lefts as rights.

At the prison, we were unshackled and made to jump down from the lorry bed. The man with the bloody shoe attempted a one-footed landing and ended up sprawled on the ground, screaming. The wet guy and I each grabbed an armpit and hoisted him to his feet, and the five of us trudged through the main gate and into the intake area. We waited for a few minutes, for the guard who would walk us back to the cells. He arrived, and we all stood up, but he motioned to me.

"You are Killy, Allain? Yes?" he said.

"Yes."

"You stay. The rest, come with me."

This was not good. It couldn't have been. Maybe Max or Rene had talked, and talked convincingly enough, that they didn't need my confirmation that I had been there to blow up the bridge. Maybe they figured the act of lopping off a few fingers or toes to confirm something they already knew to be true wasn't worth the effort. Maybe the Gestapo agent with the nippers had a full appointment book, and I just wasn't worth his time.

What was the term? Without luggage. Maybe I was without luggage.

The door opened and one of the paperwork guards from the front desk approached. He was carrying the paper parcel from my cell. Maybe I was wrong. Maybe I was with luggage, headed for a transfer to some camp. With luggage was clearly better than without luggage, but still.

"Sign here," he said, shoving a clipboard at me and pointing to a line near the bottom of a form. At the top, it said, "Release Order."

I signed. He pointed to the door.

"You are free to go," he said. He headed back to his desk, and another guard walked me out the door and then out the main gate that said "PRISON MILITAIRE" over the arch.

I was free. But why had they let me go? I should have been thrilled, but I wasn't. It didn't make any sense to me, unless they really were playing some kind of long game, just building the tension. For all I knew, they would be back at the house after we went to bed, to wake me and bring me back for more. That made some sense, but I just didn't know. I wanted to tell Manon I was okay, but didn't want to endanger her inadvertently in the process. So instead of heading west, toward our home, I headed east.

I kept a second apartment for a few reasons. Firstly, I had the money — my previous lives as an heir to a Czech magnesite mining family, and then as a bank president in Zurich, left me more than comfortable. Secondly, for operational reasons — a place to hide, or vary my routine, either before or after sabotage missions. Thirdly, it was a storage facility — extra canned food, some money, a change of clothes, a suitcase, and a couple of our passports were there, in case either Manon or I needed to make a run for it.

My landlady, Isabelle Vaillancourt, was grandly named, much grander than the premises. But the landlady, and therefore the flat, had two distinct advantages: she was 80 and almost comically deaf, which meant she was unable to hear what was happening on the floor above her and, even if she could hear, disinclined to climbing the stairs to find out. I told her I was a traveling salesman so that she wouldn't be suspicious of me spending only one or two nights a week there. The truth was, the only time I saw Isabelle was when I paid the rent.

I had been there for about an hour. I was as careful as I could be in stacking my dirty clothes in the corner of the bedroom, careful not to touch anything. I sprayed everything with some Fly-Tox that I had purchased on the walk over — it might have been the only thing in France that wasn't rationed. Then I sprayed myself, which wasn't necessarily recommended and probably was harmful, but fuck it. At least I closed my eyes and mouth. Then I took a bath, scrubbing as best as I could. I figured I got most of them, and at least stunned the rest of them.

It was there, clean and in fresh clothes, that I opened the only beer in the flat and began to consider my next move. Not five minutes after my first sip, there was a knock on the door. This was different. No one had ever knocked before.

8

I had expected it to be Isabelle. Instead, it was Leon. One of my oldest friends from Vienna was standing on the mat outside of my door. Two people were behind him, a woman and a small child, a girl who must have been seven or eight.

"Mon ami," Leon said. He had lived in Paris for the last few years, and we were speaking French.

"Fuck me," I said, hugging him. Leon was not married, and unless he had suddenly acquired a wife and child, there was a story here. He introduced his friends as Ruth, the mother, and Rachel, the child. They were from Paris. They had arrived on the train together about an hour earlier.

"Headed where?" I asked.

"South," Leon said.

"South where?"

"Just south," he said. "Very south."

Ruth and Rachel were Jewish, as was Leon. He had worked as a newspaper reporter in Vienna, and we were together on the night of the Anschluss in 1938. Leon and I and two other friends were forced to flee the Nazis for different reasons. Mine was simple enough: I was a spy for the Czech government who had tried and failed to kill a Gestapo officer in Cologne. Leon's reasons were even simpler: not only was he Jewish, but he was a Jewish journalist, which was the Nazi double-whammy. After we got over the border to Bratislava, the Czech government arranged for us to leave the country in exchange for me agreeing to run the private bank in Zurich that funded their espionage efforts. The Czechs agreed to get my friends out, too. For Leon, that meant a passport and a plane ticket to Paris, where he had a newspaper connection.

He had written at the paper until the Germans reached Paris in June of 1940, at which point the double-whammy acquired a French accent. He joined a Resistance cell almost immediately and went into hiding. One day, he sent me a letter that consisted of a date written on the top — September 9 — and a series of numbers. With it was a book, a French bible. I had described to him on a visit to Paris, just before the German invasion, the code I had used to communicate by radio with my Czech handlers. This letter and the bible suggested the same code, and I quickly deciphered it — going to page 910, which was the date plus one, and matching numbers from his letter to the sequence of letters on that page. He was providing me with the address of a bar in Paris where I could send him messages, and where I would be safe if forced to flee Lyon. I sent a reply letter, offering the address of my second apartment as a safe place for him if it came to that

We communicated infrequently after that — once-a-year infrequently. I knew how exhausting my secret life had become, and I was sure it was the same for him. Now he was in my flat with this woman and her daughter. But here's the thing: Leon was a romantic rogue of the first order, and not only was Ruth was not up to his typical standard, married-with-children had never been his style. There also was no obvious affection between Ruth and him. They had not come close to touching each other in their few minutes in my presence. His formality had been almost comical as they entered the apartment — Leon stepped aside and pointed the way ahead as if he were a maître'd at a posh restaurant. And he had never even looked at Rachel, the little girl.

"Alex, what's that smell?" Leon said.

"Fly-Tox. It's a bit of an involved story. I'll tell you later. Everybody should stay away from the clothes in the corner there, just to be safe. And in the meantime, is anyone hungry?"

Ruth said no. Rachel's eyes said yes. The cupboard was well-stocked, seeing as how one of the benefits of having more than one identity in more than one neighborhood was having a second set of ration cards. That was going to be one of the saddest parts about retiring the Allain Killy identity. I figured I was safe to collect one more set of ration cards, but that would be it. I might actually cry when I ended up burning everything.

I pulled open the cupboard door, and Ruth's eyes went wide. Leon said, "Fuck, buddy, did you rob a grocery store?"

"Another long story," I said. "In the meantime, Ruth, help yourselves."

"I couldn't," she said.

"You will and you must," I said. "Rachel, go pick out your dinner."

She ran to the cupboard and returned with a can of carrots and another can of peaches in heavy syrup. Her mother looked at me again and I said, "Just go. Anything you want — you see how much I have. Take a lot more than those two cans. I'll be insulted if you don't. You should be able to find all of the utensils you need and matches for the stove. Leon and I need to go for a walk and talk about old times."

"Save me some," he said, calling over his shoulder as we left the flat. I grabbed my last bottle of wine from a side table and followed him out.

9

A couple of blocks from the flat, on Avenue du Chateau, there was a small park below a church. We sat there, near the memorial to what was starting to be called World War I, which was our war, Leon's and mine. We were on the other side back then.

Leon extricated the cork with a penknife, and we passed the wine bottle back and forth. We hadn't done something like this since our twenties. The first time we had done it, we were both in uniform, after Caporetto, when the Italians fled down the mountain and we pillaged every wine cellar we came upon. Spoils of war and all that.

Leon raised the bottle and toasted the soldier who stood atop the memorial.

"Poor bastard," he said. "Imagine dying for a country you loved and then finding out it's all turned to shit in 20 years. I mean, what was it all for?"

He passed the bottle back, and I took a long pull. It was dark now, and people were criss-crossing the park as part of a short-cut, it seemed, rushing after work to see what they might scrounge together for dinner with whatever value was remaining on their ration cards. It was two days until the next cards, and that was always a frantic time. Just the look on some of the faces told you the strain they were under. I couldn't imagine what it would be like to go home to your kids and tell them there would be nothing to eat until the day after next.

"So what's this all about?" I said. Now it was Leon's turn to take an extra-big drink.

"They're Jews," he said.

"With the names Ruth and Rachel? You're shitting me."

"Yeah," Leon said. "That's one of the problems."

"What do you mean, problems?"

Leon sketched out the issue. The German crackdown against the Jews of Paris was increasing. There were regular roundups, and lorry-loads of Jews were being taken to what amounted to transportation hubs in and around Paris.

"One of them is called Drancy," he said. "I've seen it. They bring the Jews there and then they ship them out in railroad cars to who-knows-where. They call them 'resettlement camps' but that's all they say. They take the people and their luggage and jam them into freight cars. All we know is that the trains run to the east. And we never hear from the people again."

"Sounds very German," I said.

"Efficient as fucking clockwork."

"Are they just putting them to work somewhere?" I said.

"Nobody knows. That's what the optimists hope — cheap labor for the Nazi war machine. But I'm not much of an optimist. What about the grandmothers? Are they putting them to work in a munitions factory? What about the little kids? I try not to think about it, but it's all I can think about."

"And Ruth and Rachel?"

"The Jews who are still in Paris are completely panicked now," Leon said. "At the beginning, all we had to do was get them to the free zone. It was easy enough to hide out there."

"But not anymore," I said. "I get it. The Gestapo has been here for only a few months, and there have been roundups here — I'm not sure as many as in Paris, but it's starting." I told him about Montluc and the barracks that had been built for the Jews there.

"So you can't just go to the free zone," Leon said. "Even with that, you need a forged pass – but we were lucky with those, lucky this one time. You have to get them all the way out of the country — to Spain, and then maybe to Portugal, and then maybe out from there. But they have to get out of France, and that takes more than just money — and it takes a lot of fucking money. They're really checking the trains headed south, like toward Limoges or Bordeaux. Rachel and Ruth, it would be almost impossible for them to get to Spain directly from Paris and with their own identity papers."

"So how did you get here?"

"Lyon is south, yes," he said. "But it's southeast. It's not toward the Spanish border. And, yes, you now have your own Gestapo here. I guess they figure it's no place for a Jew to run — at least they figure that for now. They don't check the trains. So this is their opportunity."

Leon sketched out his plan, his idea of what that opportunity entailed. He wanted to smuggle Jews from Paris to the south, and he wanted to use my second flat as a way-station. He would travel with a couple of Jews from Paris to Lyon, and they would stay in my flat for a day or two and then move on south. Leon would travel with them part of the way, to make sure they got going, and then head back to Paris for the next group.

"But what about their papers?" I said. "Identity card. Travel permit. Ration cards—"

"Yeah," Leon said. "Here's my thinking. I know I didn't ask you ahead of time. It's getting harder to get the papers in Paris — the Nazis have gone after the forgers almost as hard as they've gone after the Jews — and I also can't afford it, and most of these people can't afford it. So what I was thinking was, when I bring people to the apartment, I could also bring the identities of the next group along with me, and you could maybe arrange for the paperwork with your people here."

"Oh, is that all?" I said. Leon ignored my tone.

"So then," he said, "that paperwork will be ready when the next group arrives. After a day or two, they can use it to head south, and I will have left you the identities of the next group."

"And who's paying?" I said.

Leon's eyes fell. He barely croaked out the reply.

"You have the fucking money," he said.

Of course, he was right. I did have the contacts to get the paperwork, and I did have the money. What I didn't have was the appetite for taking on an even more dangerous bit of business than blowing up the odd set of railroad tracks.

"Look," Leon said. "For whatever reason, we have this opening. The Germans might close it tomorrow. But this is a chance. I can't let it go. Just think about it. And help me get some paperwork for Ruth and Rachel to get them started south."

I agreed to think about it. We passed the wine bottle back and forth a few more times. I could help Ruth and Rachel, but I just didn't see how I could turn this into a full-time endeavor. After a silent minute or two, I changed the subject and told Leon the story of my arrest and questioning by Barbie, and then my unexpected release. He admitted that my building-the-tension theory was possible, and that he didn't have a better explanation.

But he also said, "I don't know, buddy. It sounds, I don't know, implausible. I mean, from everything I know about the Gestapo, they don't do subtlety."

Leon took the last drink from the bottle. Then he muttered, "Fuck it," and threw the empty bottle at the war memorial, shattering the glass. I looked at him and then kicked the broken glass into a pile at the base while he watched me. We walked back to my flat in silence.

"Wait," I said. We had reached the front steps of the building. "Speaking of paperwork, how are you managing to travel, Mr. Jew-from-Vienna?"

Leon reached into his pocket and smiled, handing me his identity card. I read it and burst out laughing.

"Seriously? Louis St. Jacques?" I said.

"In the fucking flesh," Leon said. "Want me to recite the Hail Mary? I've been practicing."

10

I had a key to the silk factory, but I didn't want to startle Manon by using it. So I knocked our special knock — two knocks, pause, one knock, pause, two knocks — and Leon and I waited.

Back at the apartment, the good news was that Ruth and Rachel had eaten four cans of food — carrots, new potatoes, cling peaches and pears. Rachel was asleep on the sofa, her head in Ruth's lap. Ruth was half-asleep herself when we opened the door.

Leon explained how it would go. For the next two days at least, and maybe three, Rachel and Ruth would be living alone in the flat. Either Leon or I would come by every day to check on them, but they could not leave. Even though Isabelle was deaf, they also needed to stay as quiet as possible.

"There are a couple of books on the shelf that you might like," I said to Ruth, gesturing. "I'm sorry, there isn't anything for Rachel. But there is some paper and a pencil. Maybe she could practice her drawing, or you could play some word games or something. It's the best I can do."

"It's more than enough — thank you so much," Ruth said.

"Two days, maybe three, we'll have new papers for you two," Leon said, picking up the thread. "Then I will take you to the train and we will ride together for part of the way to Toulouse. We will take local trains as much as we can, and from there, you likely will be hidden in cars or lorries to the Pyrenees. Then someone will guide you through to Spain where you will be picked up on the other side of the border."

"So many people," she said. "How—"

"Many people combatting much evil," Leon said. "They will do everything they can for you. It won't be easy, but it will work, God willing."

"God willing," Ruth whispered. It was as if she were attempting to convince herself that there was still a God after all. As we were leaving, she picked up Rachel and carried her into the bedroom.

Leon and I walked from the flat to Croix-Rousse. It took about an hour. Leon brought a can of peaches for the journey, plucking out the halves with his fingers, then drinking the sugary syrup from the can.

"Careful there," I said, as he sipped and walked. "Don't cut yourself on the rim. The girls won't like it." Leon was the kind of ladies' man they wrote books about, handsome enough but with an air about him that women seemed to find irresistible. It had been that way from the first time I met him in his teens until today.

"Girls," he said. "There are no girls. I'm too tired. Can you fucking believe it — me, too tired? I don't even try anymore."

"End of an era," I said.

"Temporary pause," he said. "Fucking Adolf."

When Manon answered the knock and unlocked the door, she was in the process of delivering a smart-ass greeting, "Sorry, but one night in jail was too much. I've found—"

She saw Leon and stopped. When I introduced them, she said, "The famous goddamn Leon." She hugged him and then held him at arm's length, looking him up and down.

"Yes, yes, I see what Alex says about you," she said. Then she looked at me and said, "Good thing he wasn't near my empty bed last night."

"My God, what did you tell her?" Leon said.

"Only the truth," I said.

"Shit," he said. Manon immediately shushed him and then hugged him again.

"Alex loves so few people, and you are clearly one of them," she said, whispering in his ear. She thought I couldn't hear, but I could. It was true. It was a very small list.

"Como in, como in, I think I can find us a bottle," Manon said, and we walked past the looms and into the back storage room that was the heart of her publishing empire. We talked about Montluc, and about Barbie, and about getting released without a scratch or a strain. She had nothing to offer as a possible explanation, either.

She was typing as she listened. The next edition of *La Dure Vérité* was already a day past the deadline she kept in her head — once every six weeks. It was a flyer, really, not a newspaper, just front and back of a single sheet and run off on the Roneo machine that was hidden in one of the crates stacked in the corner. The cranking was tiring, but for me, the reward was the smell of the still-wet sheets of paper that came out on the other side. It was intoxicating. It actually made me pleasantly dizzy.

"Do you ever need stories?" Leon asked.

"Ever? Try always. I'm short of copy now. I'm going to have to run a big blank space in this one as it is."

He pulled a notebook from his pocket.

"I was hoping you might say that," Leon said. "I wrote a little something on the train, hoping you might be able to use it. Can you read my writing?"

"This is perfect," Manon said, after a minute of scanning the notebook. "It's perfect. It's beautiful. Can I take it now?"

Leon said yes, and she started typing. It was the story of a Resistance operation, a firebombing that destroyed three dozen vehicles in the Gestapo motor pool in Paris' 3rd arrondissement. As I read over Manon's shoulder, I could tell from the text that Leon had actually been there when the explosions went off. The description was so vivid.

You smelled the fuse beforehand and the gunpowder afterward, and those were the sensations that lasted the longest. The first concussive BOOM, and the heat and the glow of the fire, and the mini-booms that followed as each of the vehicle gas tanks exploded, seemed to evaporate from my memory. But I could still smell the smells, days after and even today.

"Did you actually light the firebomb?" I said.

"One of them," he said.

"Byline?" Manon said, and Leon thought for a second.

"Just say, 'A brother from Paris.'"

"A brother from Paris it is," she said, and then the real typing began. Manon was skilled, but not like a secretary. As she worked, Leon explained what he was doing in town, and the proposal he had made about establishing an escape network for Jews that would run through my second flat. She stopped and let it all sink in.

"Leon, that's great," she said. "Alex, isn't that great?"

"It's a big risk," I said.

"But it's worth it," Manon said.

Leon looked at me, half-shrugged and said, "See?" It was clear that he figured, if it was okay with my wife, it should be okay with me. I looked at Leon, and then at Manon, and then at Leon again.

"It's not that simple," I said.

"What's not that simple?"

"Manon is pregnant," I said. "That's what's not that simple. None of this is simple anymore, if it ever was."

I was hoping that the look on my face would explain that I wasn't worrying just for one or two anymore, but for three.

11

After the ritual congratulations from Leon, there was a long silence. Manon resumed typing and finished the article quickly. Then she had me get the Roneo from the crate and set it up. She had typed on a kind of stencil, which she attached to the drum of the machine. Then I turned the crank as Leon fed the paper through. My God, that smell.

After a few minutes to dry, Manon changed to the other stencil, and we ran the paper through on the other side. Within an hour, we had 500 copies. We were waiting a few minutes for more drying when there was a knock on the door.

"You expecting anybody?" I said.

"Nope," Manon said. "What do we do?"

"Turn off the light and wait in here," I said. "I'll go see."

I rehearsed a story as I walked, something about a broken loom, but it wasn't necessary. I opened the door, and it was Max. And his first words were, "Fuck, Pops, what the fuck happened?"

I took him to the back room and introduced him to Manon and Leon. He saw the Roneo and the newly printed stack. "Nice," he said. "I knew your family owned this place — that's how I knew to come here — but I didn't know this was your print shop. But isn't that dangerous?"

"Not as long as you keep your fucking mouth shut," Manon said.

"Fuck, Pops, I like her."

We compared notes on our arrests, and Max was the winner. He didn't even make it till sunrise after we blew up the bridge.

"I was sleeping rough near the farm, like we talked about," he said. "I don't know exactly what time it was, but it was still way dark when the Gestapo showed up. I thought I was going to be okay until I heard the barking. The dogs sniffed me out in about two minutes."

So now they had dogs. The idea of sleeping out in the open near transit contacts would have to be re-thought. We would need to create more distance, better safeguards. The operations were hard enough, but cat-and-mouse — the thinking in between missions — was somehow even more exhausting.

"I think I saw Rene in Montluc," I said. "Did you?"

"No. Fuck."

"Exactly," I said. "Fuck."

"But how did they find all three of us?" Max said. "I got caught, but I didn't tell. They barely did anything. I mean, they slapped me around a little bit, and I denied everything, and then they let me go." He stopped, and pulled back his hair, and pointed to a one-inch gash along his hairline.

"But that was it," he said. "I mean, it was nothing."

"And when and where did they question you?" I said.

"The next day, at the Gestapo place on Avenue Berthelot. It was after I had a nice sleep in that fucking hole and two gourmet meals. They took me down the basement, and did what they did, and then sent me back. The other guys in the truck got it much worse."

"So I had already been arrested before they even questioned

you," I said. It was a kind of thinking-out-loud statement. I was hoping someone would jump in with a brilliant insight. Instead, there was only silence, followed by Max's predictable, "Fuck."

We sat for a few more minutes, sorting out nothing. Then Manon said, "Look, we need to get these on the night train to Grenoble. There's a conductor who will take them, and we have a taxi driver who will bring them to the station. The taxi will be waiting at the Rue de Capucins."

"I know the way," I said.

"You need a little more practice in the traboules — bring Max," Manon said. "You're from the neighborhood, right?"

Max agreed, and Leon insisted on tagging along for the experience. It was into a light rain that the three of us began to walk. Max carried the small cardboard suitcase containing the flyers. It was past curfew, which meant the risk was significant if a random Gestapo patrol happened upon us. And while it wasn't as if they had the manpower — yet — to really turn the screws and keep the streets completely empty at night, the consequences of getting caught were another trip to Montluc. I really didn't need that.

It was about a block from the first traboule entrance when we saw the headlights, maybe three blocks in the distance. "Run," Max said, and we did. We approached a random doorway on Rue Imbert Colomes. The little sign out front said it was No. 20.

"Quick, this way," Max said. "Will you and your fucking friend hurry up, Pops?"

We ducked into the doorway at No. 20. As the door slammed behind us the passageway, maybe 20 feet long, was completely dark. Then we reached a staircase going down, maybe 20 steps, each of smooth stone. The top of the staircase was covered but the bottom few steps were wet from the rain that was falling into the open courtyard, the area surrounded by the six-story apartment houses that provide its form. There was a black iron railing on the left side of the step. Down at the bottom, you could see the ivy growing up along its latticework. Looking quickly at it, I lost my concentration and stumbled on the ceramic down near the bottom of the steps. Then I fell. Max put down the suitcase and helped me up.

"Goddamn fucking old man," he said. "Are you all right?"

"I'm fine."

"Everything except your dignity," Leon said.

"Look, just fuck both of you." It was the best I could do.

Leon looked around as I got myself together. We were getting wet. He said, "But I thought these things were built to protect the silk from being damaged by rain when it was being transported to the river."

"That's clearly bullshit," Max said. "I don't know why, but they've been here since the Middle Ages. I think it's mostly for this. You know, the clandestine. Come."

What we were doing was cutting through anonymous passageways between and among the apartment buildings, which allowed you to go down from the hills of Croix-Rousse without being on the streets very much.

There were four doorways in this first traboule. Three led to staircases up to the flats. The fourth, leading to another street, is where we went. Max opened the door just wide enough to stick his head out and look both ways for more headlights. "Come," he said again.

We end up doing this four times, making our way down from the hills. The only times we were on the streets were the quick crossing of the narrow roads, maybe 50 feet between the houses on either side, 50 feet on Rue des Tables Claudiennes, 50 more feet on Rue Burdeau, and finally 50 feet on another street I didn't know. Then we exited the fifth traboule on Rue de la Capucins. It was five minutes before 11. The taxi was waiting at the door we came out of, No. 6. He took the suitcase without a word and drove off in the direction of the station.

The handoff was the easy part. The hard part would be retracing our steps, back through the same traboules, but uphill this time instead of downhill. We were exhausted, but at least we didn't see another set of headlights the rest of the night.

12

I still hadn't agreed to participate in Leon's scheme, but Ruth and Rachel were here, in my other flat, and they needed new papers to continue their journey. We were so tired when we got back to the house that we didn't talk about it anymore, and Manon was already asleep.

"Let's just sleep as long as we can and get the papers for them when we wake up," I said, and Leon agreed. As it turned out, we both slept until almost noon, me with Manon, and Leon in our second bedroom. She was up early and neither of us heard a thing.

We awoke to a feast of the little bit of food that we had left in the house, this being the last day before the new ration cards came out. Technically, it was half of what we had left — the other half would be dinner. Seeing as how she was pregnant — four months pregnant but still not showing — Manon qualified for a more generous allotment than I did. But it still wasn't nearly enough. Breakfast — and dinner — would be slices from a semi-stale baguette, fried in lard and topped with white beans that had been fried in the same pan. Dessert was an apple, split three ways. Leon and I drank fake coffee, which really tasted like strained shit, but it was all there was. Manon drank the last of the milk I had brought from the farm.

After we ate, Manon went to the factory to put in a couple of hours of bookkeeping. Leon and I walked into the center of town, but this time on the streets and not in the traboules, down the hills, down the staircases, down, down, down.

At the Hotel de Ville, we passed the enormous fountain that anchored the square in front of it. The enormous fountain was topped by a naked woman on a chariot with enormous naked breasts. I pointed them out to Leon, and he stopped and stared.

"The old me would have made a comment, like those kids," he said, gesturing toward a couple of 12-year-old boys who were pointing and snickering in the way that every pair of 12-year-old boys in the last half-century had done as they passed the fountain. "But I'm too tired now, even for massive iron breasts."

"I think they're lead," I said.

"Like there's a difference. Only you would know that."

"I read it in one of the papers, back before they were censored," I said. "The same article today would say they were massive German breasts."

A block or two on the other side of the big square was Rue du Garet, a little street with a couple of quiet shops. One had stenciled in the window, "Stamps, Coins, Collectibles." The proprietor was Marcel Roux. I don't know if his stamp or coins or collectibles were worth shit, but Marcel was the best forger in Lyon, one of only three in the city who were part of the Resistance.

He had made both of my fake identities, and one for Manon, too. He wasn't cheap — or, as he said, "I have to pay people to steal the blank paper, and that doesn't cost nothing, you know." But he really was the best. I had never gotten a passport from him, and didn't know about that, but as for identity cards and transit papers, he was the best. You really couldn't tell his from the real thing.

The identity cards had a lot going on — the correct stock was important, and the red border needed to be the proper shade, and the photo and the various stamps from the police and the rest were all required. Every detail had to be right, and Marcel's identity cards were right. No one ever got caught because of that.

"Only time someone got caught, it wasn't my fault," Marcel said. It was a story he told every time I had been in his shop, and he was telling it again to me and Leon now, after I made the introductions.

"The fool who I made the card for, he filled it out wrong. He put his birth date in the spot where it said to put in the issue date. Idiot. He deserved to get caught."

We explained to Marcel what we needed — new identity cards for Ruth and Rachel, with Gentile names and untraceable details.

"You have the photos?" Marcel asked. Leon handed them over. He had taken them himself. His last act as a big city newspaperman was to liberate from the paper's photo department a sufficient supply of chemicals to develop a few hundred small identity card photos. He had dozens already posed and taken and developed back in Paris.

"Okay, let me check my book," Marcel said. While his craftsmanship was impressive, his research abilities were unmatched. Through a military source — he would never tell who it was — Marcel had obtained a list of the cities and towns whose records offices were destroyed during the German invasion in 1940. What that meant was, the Gestapo did not have the ability to check an identity card from those places. If the card appeared to be legitimate, there was nothing to do but accept it. There was no way to prove from existing records that it was a forgery because the records just didn't exist anymore. The panzers had blown them away.

"I need to rotate these around," he said, running his finger down a list of names. "Too many in a short period from the same place could be risky. Okay, they will be from Pleau Est. It's up near Amiens. Little farming town. Germans bombed the shit out of it. You think the little girl can remember that much?"

Both Leon and I thought that she could.

"Two days?" I said.

"Phew," Marcel said. "I don't know—"

"I can pay a little extra," I said, counting out the bills on his workbench. He scooped them up and dropped them into the same drawer where he kept his book of bombed-out records offices.

"I have a question," Leon said. "If we were to bring you business of this type on a regular basis, could you handle it with the same fast turnaround?"

"We're not sure yet," I said.

"Two or three names, maybe twice a month," Leon said.

"Really, we're not sure."

"Right now, I can handle that," Marcel said. "But you never know. Life around here gets more complicated all the time. And if the paper supply dries up, we're out of business. You understand that, right?"

"Sure, sure," Leon said.

"As long as you understand, then yes," Marcel said.

"But we're really not sure," I said.

As we turned to leave, Marcel cleared his throat. He was nothing if not theatrical, and also single-minded. The final part of every under-the-table transaction in his shop was an actual transaction, so that if the Gestapo began to suspect, and stopped us outside, we would have a purchase to show them. So I bought the cheapest old nineteenth-century franc I could find in the display case.

"Ah, nice choice," Marcel said. "It is just for operational integrity, you know." He wrote out a receipt, and then he opened the drawer of his workbench and scooped the payment inside.

13

Every month, Isabelle made me a pie. Where she got the ingredients was one of the great mysteries of my current life. Flour, sugar, fat and the fruit filling — all in the early spring of 1943; I had no idea. Its arrival, sitting there on my doormat, was unpredictable but predictable, if that made any sense. Every month, at some point but always a different point, it was there. And so it was on that day.

Leon had begged off after our visit to Marcel's shop. He said he couldn't make the walk over to the flat.

"I'm just exhausted," he said. "If it's okay with you, I just want to go back to your house and sleep some more. Just the idea of walking back up those hills has me even more tired. I don't know, I'm just spent."

So he went back, and I came to the flat to check on Ruth and Rachel, and the pie was the great bonus. I did the math in my head as soon as I picked it up to smell it — cherry. A slice each for Ruth and Rachel, and a slice each for Manon, the baby in her belly, Leon and I, left two more. And it gave me an idea. After checking on Ruth and Rachel, and watching Rachel's delight at the sight of some actual dessert, I carefully wrapped the four slices for us in one piece of butcher paper and the other two slices in another piece.

"Any news?" Ruth said. Rachel dived face-first into her portion, and we walked toward the door.

"I can't stay," I said. Then I told her about the paperwork, about the quality of the forger, and about the cover story.

"I'll begin practicing with her," Ruth said. "Pleau Est. Near Amiens. We lived on a farm."

"She'll be okay with it, won't she?"

"Yes, yes," Ruth said. "I'll make it like a game. I just won't tell her that the losers get killed."

"Does she understand any of this?"

"Not really," she said. "She knows that there are bad people who don't like us, so we're going to a place where the bad people don't live. That seems to be enough for her."

Ruth stopped for a second, hesitated, then said, "She doesn't cry at night. I'm the one that cries at night."

Which was a hell of an au revoir. I left them there, with their pie and their preoccupations, and walked to Montluc. I wanted to see if Rene was still there. This whole thing was steeped in illogic. I know I didn't give anybody up to the Gestapo. I know Max didn't give me up, seeing as how he wasn't questioned until after I was arrested. That left Rene. And while he didn't seem the type, well, who exactly was the type? And when they started lopping off your fingers, who among us would hold out?

As I approached the window — it was like a window at a bakery — I was hoping to talk to Charles. He wasn't exactly a guard at the prison, but he was more than a custodian. It was hard to explain, and I listened to him try once at a Friere family gathering — he was a second cousin to Manon, or maybe something even more distant than that. Anyway, I knew he worked the window sometimes when people brought packages for prisoners, and I was due a bit of luck. When I rang the little bell, the shutters opened, and it was, indeed, Charles who answered. It took a second for my face to register with him.

"I heard you were here," he said, after first looking back over his shoulder. There was no one there. "Actually, I saw you. Allain Killy, huh? How did you like our little country inn, Monsieur Killy?"

"I had a splendid night in the Shithole Arms," I said. And then Charles looked over his shoulder again.

"Yeah, I heard they let you go pretty quick, too," he said. "And that you were still pretty as ever when you left. That's exactly what one of the drivers said, 'pretty as ever.' I mean, you look like crap to me, but that's what he said."

"Is that unusual?" I said.

"Very. The typical guy, we take him to Avenue Berthelot and he at least gets beat up. Maybe a quarter lose a finger or a toe — but that's usually on the second day, after they get roughed up on the first. Then there are the ones we never see again. There's a few of them. More than a few."

I thought some more about the whole business on the walk over and massaged the idea that maybe they were laying a trap for me, hoping to catch me in some bigger scheme. But I wasn't being followed, which you would have thought was a prerequisite for that kind of plan. I was careful that way. Years of doing this — starting as a spy for the Czechs in 1938 — had taught me a few things and spotting a tail was one of them. I did all of the necessary mechanics — circuitous routes, doubling back, checking in the plate glass of storefronts as if they were mirrors, all of that — and I was clean. Besides, I really didn't think the Gestapo had that kind of manpower in Lyon. Not yet, anyway.

Every explanation I came up with, I just as quickly found a hole in the theory. It was driving me insane. Maybe that was the purpose. I mean, I just didn't know.

Charles began to look antsy. I held up the smaller of my two parcels. I wanted to leave it for Rene. Mostly, I wanted to find out if Rene was still in Montluc. Charles left the window and walked back into the office to check.

"Sorry," he said. "He's not here."

"Can you find—"

"No, I can't. And I can't be talking to you like this. It'll seem suspicious if any of my bosses comes along. And let me tell you, I've got bosses out the ass in this place."

"German bosses?"

"Not yet, but that's the rumor," he said.

"When?"

"Soon," he said.

"Okay, one last thing. Instead of Rene, can I leave this for the kid who was in the same cell with me the night I was here? I don't know his name, but he looked like he was about 17."

"Christ," Charles said. "All right. Hang on — but this is it."

He went back and checked. As it turned out, my young friend was still in the same cell. I asked Charles for a pencil, and I wrote a short note on the butcher paper that was wrapped around the two slices of cherry pie. A little bit of the filling had leaked out, and the paper was stained red in one corner.

The note said, "Sorry, but I couldn't find any apples this time."

14

We ate the pie before we ate the dinner — one slice each for Leon and I, two for Manon, although she did give us each a forkful from her second slice. "Please, please," she said. "It's still a tiny baby."

After that, the fried bread and beans were an anticlimax, but in a world where all gratification seemed to be delayed — that is, when it wasn't non-existent — we couldn't possibly deny ourselves. I didn't actually lick the pie plate because that would have been uncouth. But I did wipe the plate repeatedly and lick my forefinger after each pass. Leon hesitated for a second and then did the same. Then Manon followed along. As she said, "Classy is as classy does."

After we cleaned up properly, Leon announced that he was still exhausted and heading back to bed. Between his previous night's sleep and his afternoon nap, Leon had already clocked about 15 hours in the rack, and it was only 9 p.m. Manon looked at me a little crooked and then just blurted out, "Are you okay? Do you think you're sick?"

"Okay is a relative term, I think," he said. "I'm not okay. I can't believe the world I live in. I can't believe I'm trying to smuggle this nice woman and her innocent little daughter out of the country because that's the only way to keep the government from killing them, or putting them on a train to God-knows-where. So, no, I'm not okay."

He stopped himself.

"I don't mean to sound harsh," he said. "I know I'm not alone in this. And I don't think I'm sick and thank you for being worried. But I just feel so stretched, stretched beyond any limits I thought I had. But you know what? Coming here, this is the first time I've felt safe in a very long time, and I think my adrenaline — and I've been living on adrenaline — has stopped being produced because I finally feel safe. So I'm just going to go back to sleep."

He wasn't two steps out of the kitchen when Manon said, "Well, I'm glad somebody feels safe."

"He told me a little about what he's been doing," I said. "He's writing for an underground paper. He's secretly delivering the paper. He's been trying to organize this Jewish transport scheme. He spends most nights sleeping on a couch in the basement of a bar where he often hangs out. He's afraid to go home to his own flat for any length of time. He said to me, 'I'm eating like shit, I'm not getting enough rest, I'm drinking too much, I've been close to being arrested a dozen times, and I have nobody to talk to after the lights are off.'"

By this time, we were on the couch in the living room. The lights were off. I said a little prayer — not exactly my style — that I would always have somebody to talk to when the lights were off, both Manon and the tiny life in her belly.

I put my hand there, hoping to feel a kick or something, but all was quiet. Then I remembered.

"Oh, shit, the doctor. I completely forgot. Tell me."

"Not much to tell," Manon said. "All good."

"Nothing?"

"He listened and heard a heartbeat. He let me listen, too. It's there. There's a little Alex in there. Or Alexandra."

"Hell no. Give the kid a chance. Name him after somebody else."

"I'll think about it."

"Did the doctor say anything else?"

"Just eat and rest," Manon said.

"New coupons tomorrow," I said. "We'll have a feast."

"Great. More rutabagas. Can't wait. I swear to God, when this is all over, I'm never going to eat another rutabaga again."

"What about Jerusalem artichokes?"

"Them too," she said. "My God, how could we have so many of those damn things but no fresh green beans? No asparagus? I would kill for a spear. Just one."

We settled into a silence, my arm around Manon's shoulder, her head laying down on my chest. We were both avoiding the subject of Leon's scheme for transporting Jews to Spain. Some couples finished each other's sentences after a while. Manon and I could read each other's silences. It was almost telepathic. As soon as I started thinking about Ruth and Rachel in the flat, Manon began talking about it.

"So why are you reluctant?" She didn't have to elaborate.

"I don't know," I said. "It's not the money."

"I never thought it was the money."

"It's just the—"

"The what?"

"The danger," I said.

"You blow up bridges, for God's sake. You spied for your country. You tried to kill a Gestapo officer in Cologne. You killed a Nazi spy in Zurich. You joined the Resistance here without a second's hesitation."

She was right, but she couldn't see it. How she couldn't see it was beyond me.

"I used to be a physical coward," I said. "I'm still cautious about things — you know that. You know I insist on running my own sabotage operations or I won't do them. It's because I'm careful. It's because I don't trust many people. And Leon's plan, it just very dangerous."

Then I put my hand on Manon's belly.

"My life is already risky enough," I said. "This would double the risk. Maybe triple. I can't even calculate it, which scares me."

"You calculate too much?" she said.

"What, did we just meet? Is this just dawning on you?"

I patted her stomach.

"My life is crazily dangerous right now," I said. "With the baby, how can I add new layers of risk, many new layers? How can I do that with a clear conscience? We both run risks because we believe in our cause. We are taking risks to fight evil, and there is no greater reason. There is no more noble cause. But how can I add new risks, incalculable risks, with that baby growing bigger every day in your stomach? When is enough, enough?"

Again, the silence fell between us. It really wasn't that I was scared. I had been scared before, earlier in my life — scared about what other people thought about me, and just a physical coward sometimes. That was the past, though, and I guess I had Adolf to thank. This really was about Manon, and especially about the baby.

We were half-dozing when Manon spoke up. Her voice was quiet, sleepy.

"I can't tell you what to do," she said. "And I'm not going to bring it up again, whatever you decide. I understand the risks, and you'll be the one taking them, and it's not my place to make this decision."

Her voice cracked, and she jammed her head a little deeper into my chest. And then Manon said, "I love you, and I love your concern for me and our baby. And I know this is a confusing time because it's confusing for me, too. But some things are really very clear to me, and this is one of them. I believe that a child without a father is a great sadness. But I also believe that a child without freedom is a tragedy."

I had no answer for that. I wasn't sure that I agreed with her. I wasn't sure about anything. After a minute, I lifted Manon and carried her into the bedroom and placed her on her side of the bed. We both fell asleep within seconds, it seemed, still wearing our clothes.

15

R   achel was in the kitchen. Leon had found her some crayons and a coloring book, and she was determined to color in every page, it seemed.

"She appears driven," I said.

"That's her," Ruth said. "That's my Rachel. She starts something, she finishes it. I just wish I had another coloring book. This one won't last the rest of the day."

"How is she with the story?" Leon said.

"Better than I am," Ruth said. "She really has accepted it as a kind of game and has been adding new details all the time. How many cows? Three. What color is the house? White. What color is the barn? Red. What is our crop? Beans. What are the cows' names? Blackie, Brownie and Little Brownie. She is quite the little liar. Has me a little worried, to be honest."

"And the name?" I said.

"She loves it. She went to sleep singing it, Rosemarie Belmont. She likes it better than Rachel Berger, I'm pretty sure."

"And you, Roxanne Belmont?"

"Not so much," she said.

It had been four days altogether. Marcel came through with

the identity cards, and they really were impossible to distinguish from the real thing. The first and last initials were the same as their real ones, which would take care of any laundry marks or other monograms.

"But where are the old ones?" Ruth said.

"It's not safe to keep them," I said.

"But that means I can never be Ruth anymore? And there can be no Rachel anymore?"

"Only on paper," Leon said.

"I guess," Ruth said.

The truth was a little more complicated. It was true that it would not be safe for Ruth and Rachel to be carrying two sets of papers. The discovery of the old set during a routine Gestapo search of their belongings would result in an instant arrest. But it also was true that there was a kind of code within the Resistance, that the forger kept the old paperwork to use it in any way possible for a future forgery. It was a pay-it-forward ethos, but it was hard to explain to people who already were paying so much. For them, the simple explanation worked best.

Rachel ran to the table to show off the latest page she had finished. It was, in fact, a farm with three cows, one black and two brown. She showed each of us in turn, and accepted our praise, and then scampered back to the kitchen table to begin another page.

"Can we go through it again," Ruth said. "I'm sorry, b—"

"Nothing to be sorry about," Leon said.

"—but I just need to hear it again. What, for the fifth time?"

"Sixth," Leon said, adding as big a smile as he could muster. Another little laugh from Ruth was the reply.

With that, Leon again recited the details of the plan. He had already purchased the train tickets, three third-class seats on the 6:35 p.m. train to Toulouse. It was a local train that would stop a million times and took nearly three times as long as the daily express. If the Gestapo asked, they took the local to save money. But the truth was, the Gestapo pretty much never cared who was getting on the locals.

From what Leon and the Resistance had seen — and our cell had bribed a conductor based in Lyon and contributed some to that information — the Gestapo presence was concentrated along the southern border with Spain, along the Atlantic coast, and in the bigger cities. Lyon, the second biggest city in the country, was one of those larger concentrations — and a hearty welcome to you, Klaus Barbie. But even then, they didn't have the personnel to search every train. So they concentrated on the links between the bigger cities, and especially on the trains to Limoges and Bordeaux. But outside of those cities, and away from the coast, and before you got to the Pyrenees in the south, there was a vast area that was still mostly policed by the donkeys employed by Vichy. So as long as you stayed on the local trains, and stayed away from Limoges and Bordeaux, you were relatively safe. At least, that was the theory.

"I'll take you part of the way," Leon said. "And when you get to Toulouse, you will be met by a different group from the Resistance. Just walk out of the station, out of the main entrance, and they will approach you."

"And then what?" Ruth said.

"The rest of the journey could be in the boot of a car," Leon said. "It could be in the back of a farm wagon. It could be on foot. It could be on another local train for a while. The people there will choose the safest mode of transportation. But you should probably count on going the last few kilometers on foot. We are fortunate to have a lot of old Basque smugglers working for our side. They've been sneaking in and out of Spain for centuries."

"I don't know how to thank you," she said.

"Thank us when you get there," Leon said. And then he

looked at me and signaled toward the door. He wanted to have a private conversation.

"More old times to talk about?" Ruth said.

"Something like that," Leon said.

"If you hear me scream, come save me," I said.

We sat on the front steps of the building. It was almost dark. They would have to leave for the station in a few minutes.

"So," Leon said. One word, and it said everything. One word, and it encapsulated the entire debate. I had decided one way and then the other way in the hours since I woke up. Manon had kept her word and not brought it up during breakfast. Leon had finally refreshed himself and left the house early. Back and forth, back and forth — and then, every time she stood up in the kitchen, I tried to see if there was even the hint of a pregnant belly on Manon yet. But there wasn't.

I'm not sure I decided until Leon spoke up. And into the silence, he repeated, "So..."

"Fuck it, I'm in."

He started crying. I told him, "Stop fucking crying." He put his head in both hands, and I said, "You know, I can still change my mind."

We talked a little about what would come next. Leon figured he would be back in Paris in a week, and then he would take a day or two to recharge and organize the next group, or maybe more.

"I'm going to have to come up with different routes to Lyon, just to avoid running into the same Gestapo asshole by accident at the station. You know, maybe go north first, then south. Maybe a car out to the suburbs and then train after that. It'll take me a while to work it all out."

He figured he would be back in about three weeks. He said I should try to relax between now and then, and then check the flat every day after that.

"If you look at it that way, I'm only putting your life at risk one week out of four," he said. "Two, tops."

"I feel much better now," I said.

He reached into his breast pocket and handed me an envelope.

"What's this?" I said. "I told you, I would handle the money."

"It isn't money. It's the identity information and the photographs for the next group."

"Motherfucker," I said. "You knew I was going to agree all along. How did you know if I didn't?"

"I was 90 percent sure," Leon said. "I was 99 percent sure after I met Manon. Never forget what a lucky jerk you are. Ten years ago, it would have been zero percent. You would have blown it off and booked your next sales trip to Dusseldorf and come back with a funny story about how drunk the factory owner got at lunch. Zero percent. But my little boy, he's all grown up now."

"Motherfucker," I said. Then I was the one who was crying.

PART II

16

The basement of a brothel was where the semi-regular meetings of the Lyon Resistance Consortium met. I made up that name. It didn't really have a name. It was just the leaders of the different Resistance groups in the city who decided that they needed to join together soon after the Gestapo came to town — but it all happened above our heads. Manon didn't really know the details.

The brothel didn't have a name on the door, but everyone knew it as Delilah's. It had been a going concern for long enough that the place was run by the second generation — by Delilah's daughter, Eve. Except everybody called her Delilah all the same. It was a tiny place by the standards of the industry, only four bedrooms. The Germans took their business elsewhere, without exception, partly because it was such a small place but mostly because it wasn't near the center of the city where the Gestapo did most of its work and where its soldiers mainly were bedded down in hotels that had been requisitioned.

So Delilah's was a place where a Resistance fighter on the run could hide out for a couple of days without being caught. No one had ever been spotted going in or going out, to the best of our knowledge. And the basement was big enough to hold the 20 or so leaders of the various Resistance groups when a meeting was necessary.

This meeting was called in the week after the arrests of Rene, Max and me, but that wasn't the stated reason. It was just an "operational update," whatever that was. Each cell was allowed two members at the meeting, which meant Manon and I out of our little group of six. And if some of them resented how much space we took up given our size — and they did — well, fuck them. Because they all knew, however small we were, that we punched above our weight. Our newspaper was better-written than most of their shit, and they knew what they were doing when they chose me to lead more than my share of sabotage operations. Yes, fuck them — even as the tone of the meeting grew tense, and the subject of our arrests came up.

"Wait, wait," I said, interrupting a half-dozen people asking questions. "I've seen Max. He got out right after me. But has anybody seen Rene?"

Everybody looked at each other and shrugged. His people, from *Combat* — every group took the name of its newspaper — said they had not heard. I told them that I went to Montluc and was told he wasn't there. I said, "That leaves Avenue Berthelot, or..."

There was no need to finish the thought.

"Who was arrested first?" It was a guy from *Liberation*, a particular prick who had once put his hand on Manon's ass when I was away on a mission. She delighted in telling me how she nearly snapped it off at the wrist.

"Don't know," I said. "From what Max says, he was arrested about six hours after we blew up the bridge. I was arrested about 24 hours after. I have no idea about Rene."

More conversation filled the room — actually, about six

conversations at once. Everybody was worried about a leak of some sort. From one of the conversations, I heard nothing but the term "double-agent." There was a sufficient number of people who would not look me in the eye that I noticed. I mean, I knew that some of them wondered a bit, given the piece of my background that they knew, given the German flavor to my French pronunciations, but I had proven myself to them a dozen times over. More. And there were enough people who did look me in the eye, so I wasn't really worried. Well, not that worried.

Eventually, the conversations petered out, and the topic turned to Barbie. One guy — I didn't know who he was, or what group he represented — had become friends with a file clerk at Avenue Berthelot. He had learned some background over the last couple of weeks and stood on a chair to recite it from a sheet of paper.

"Klaus Barbie," he said. "Born October 25, 1913, in Bad Godesberg. Joined the SS in 1935. Worked for a time for the SD, in intelligence. Became a Nazi Party member on May 1, 1937. Party number 4,583,085."

Booing and cursing flared and then quickly died down. He continued reading.

"Barbie was assigned to Amsterdam sometime after Holland fell, probably in 1941. He was assigned to Dijon in 1942. We all know that he arrived here on November 11, 1942. That's all I have."

All of this information was both interesting and useless, but it managed to spark another half-dozen conversations, with nearly 20 people talking at once and nobody listening to more than one other person amid the din. The whole thing was pointless. There was no way that the Resistance was ever going to be a cohesive unit. It made sense to band together for operations, for coordination reasons and manpower reasons, but the rest of this was just a bullshit attempt at camaraderie. I mean, there was no way I was ever going to be friends with some of those people, especially the Communists. And the truth was, most of them were Communists.

As Manon said, "You can dismiss them out of hand, but we wouldn't exist as a movement without them. They're used to being organized in secret. They bring men, and they bring passion."

"And they bring lunacy."

"Not all of them," she said. "Your little friend Max—"

"He's too young to be a Communist. He doesn't know shit about anything."

"If you say so," Manon said.

This little private conversation, like the rest of the meeting, was going nowhere. At the hint of a suggestion from the group that the meeting was over, Manon and I were the first ones out the door and up the stairs from the cellar. It was 15 minutes until the curfew, and we would be home with a minute or two to spare if we hurried. But even if we were late, and even if we got stopped, it was unlikely any policeman or Gestapo soldier was going to trouble himself with a man and his pregnant wife. On some level, even those who worked on the side of evil were like the rest of us. Arrests meant paperwork, and the key part of paperwork was work, and who wanted to make unnecessary work for themselves?

On the way out, Manon asked Delilah, "Are these meetings good for business?"

"Better than you think," she said.

17

Raymond was a Lyon cop. He didn't work for the Gestapo or for the Vichy government. He was a municipal police officer — in his words, "just a fucking flatfoot."

Raymond also was another of Manon's second cousins. Unlike Charles, the one who worked behind the window at Montluc, we were actual friends with Raymond, not just acquaintances from a family reunion. Raymond and Manon had been close as kids and stayed that way as adults. He and his wife, Marie, had been to our house for dinner many times, and they had reciprocated. Their kids called us Uncle Alex and Aunt Manon. Lucy, their littlest, rode on my back as if I were a horse, rode until I was exhausted. When I collapsed, she would be inconsolable — so I always found a little more energy for one more trip around the perimeter of the living room.

But we had seen less of them since the Gestapo arrived in town, to protect both of us. Raymond knew about our work with the Resistance and just felt it made sense to create some distance between us, and we didn't disagree. So this meeting, which was arranged by me leaving a bit of a cryptic note for him at his precinct, was at night. And it was at the site of the Roman ruins, up in the hills of the old town.

Lyon was an old Roman outpost, and in the years before the German invasion, archaeologists had discovered the ruins, including a huge amphitheater. To get there, I rode the funicular up to the site. It was a short ride, only a couple of minutes. I picked it up at Vieux Lyon station, and it was only one car, just me and the driver. It was a pretty safe bet I wasn't being followed.

The car rose up among the rooftops at an impressively sharp angle. It struggled with the steepness but you never got the impression it was going to slip. And even if it did struggle, the alternative was to walk my lazy ass about a half-mile, maybe more, pretty much straight uphill on Montee St. Bartalmey. It wasn't worth the energy if you didn't have to do it. At least it wasn't worth it to me.

The amphitheater was across the street from Minimes station, almost directly. The excavation and preservation of the ruin was, like everything, stopped in time. The work had continued assiduously until 1940. But it was as if every clock in France stopped that spring.

There were actually two theaters in the complex, but one was clearly the more impressive. A path of rough, huge cobbles from Roman times showed the way. It was very easy to sprain an ankle, especially in the dark. Running away from someone, down this path, would be suicide for some ligament or other. Maybe you could see your way down in a full moon. Maybe. And if they were wet, these stones smoothed by nearly two centuries of foot traffic would be like ice.

You could see what the archaeologists had uncovered, more than the bare outlines. There was a stage at the bottom, and what appeared to be an area of preferred seating right in front. Then came row after stone row, 26 rows in all, each one steeply stacked upon the rest. It wasn't hard to imagine a performance taking place, actors on the stage, a couple of thousand people straining to hear — although the theory was that, once the excavation was complete, the legendary acoustics of these amphitheaters would be revealed.

In the back, behind the theater, the archaeologists had discovered a system of alleyways leading down to the theater from the town. But the alleys were not all connected. Whether that was because of the decay of the years, or because the archeologists hadn't yet connected them, was unclear. Whatever, the result was a series of dead-ending little passageways, likely built around the time of Christ's birth, whose primary purpose in the 1940s was a place for teenagers to have sex. Or for Resistance members to meet with each other. Or, in this case, to meet with a fucking flatfoot named Raymond.

"Over here," he said, and I walked into one of the dead-ending passageways. We were surrounded by 2,000-year-old stone and mortar.

"Before you talk, listen," Raymond said. "If another cop shows up, the story is that I was on a night patrol and you were a fag getting a blowjob, and that the other guy got away but that you couldn't run because your pants were around your ankles. Then he and I will have a good laugh, and I'll let him hit you with his nightstick, and then I'll hit you. His might hurt, but I'll make sure only to get you in the shoulder. Then we'll let you leave."

"You have thought this through," I said. "Why can't it be a woman giving me a blowjob?"

"It's a better story my way."

"Better for who?"

We both laughed, and then we caught up with family details. I told him Manon was pregnant, and he told me Marie was pregnant again with their third, and I said, "What are we, idiots? There isn't enough food as it is."

"I bet the birth rate is going to be up since the Gestapo got here," Raymond said. "I mean, what else is there to do at night?"

He started talking about his job. He said the Gestapo had changed that, too.

"Why? Are they up your ass?" I said.

"Really the opposite," he said. "They have taken all the major crimes — like, they investigate every murder. I guess they want to see if it's somehow tied to the Resistance. They obviously take any bombing or sabotage or major theft of something they might classify as 'war materials.' And then, well, just think about it. Think about what life is like around here now. People never go out at night. There really isn't anything left to steal — except food and ration cards, and even the crooks think it's shitty to steal somebody's ration cards. It's pretty hard to get drunk anymore, and because of that, domestic calls are way down. There just isn't a lot happening, except for people robbing food stores — and I'll be damned if I'm going to chase those down, or at least not very hard. I spend part of a lot of shifts directing traffic."

He stopped, laughed. "I kind of wish I caught you getting a blowjob, Alex. I mean, it would be tough for Manon, but it would give me something to do. I haven't made an arrest all week."

Then we got down to the purpose of the meeting. I told Raymond about the new venture Leon and I were embarking on. He listened, nodded a little warily. Raymond was not that different from me. He was calculating the angles.

"So what do you need from me?" he said.

"I don't know. Probably nothing. Hopefully nothing. But—"

"So I don't get it."

It was hard to explain, but I tried. The thing that scared me the most about the operation was that I didn't have control — or, at least, not enough control. I was providing the dormitory, and the paperwork, and the money to buy the paperwork for the Jews being smuggled. But the rest was Leon's, and that scared me. He didn't know the city, and he was temperamentally more reckless than I was. It was a temperament that had served him well, but the stakes were higher now. And I was as much at risk as he was. Considering Manon and the baby, I had much more to lose.

"I'm not sure," I said. "And I know it isn't fair to ask. But if I sense trouble, and I have a feeling that you might be able to help somehow, I want to be able to contact you — to talk, to run my ideas by you, to see if you have any ideas. So I need to be able to signal you."

"So just call me," he said.

"Too dangerous."

"Leave a note at the station, like today."

"Too dangerous."

"For who?" Raymond said.

I didn't answer. The truth was, if the Gestapo was on to me, anybody who came near me would be suspect. What if they were on to me and I didn't know? In the silence that followed his question, Raymond processed all of this without me having to say anything more. He thought for a second.

"Fuck," he said. "Okay. What? What's the signal?"

I told him that there was a black lamppost directly across the street from the front door of his police precinct. I would make an X about three feet from the bottom with yellow chalk. If it was there in the morning, he would meet me at the Roman amphitheater at 9 o'clock that night.

18

W hen Leon left Lyon the last time, the envelope he left me contained five photos and information for five identity cards. He explained that three would be coming with him on the next trip, and we would swap out their old identities for their new ones at the flat. But he said that the more he thought about it, the ideal situation would be to make the swap at the start, in Paris. So the other identity cards would be for the next two, a mother and son. From then on, the plan would be to obtain the new identity cards for the next group during the two- or three-day wait in the flat with the current group. There would be a risk in carrying them back, but it would be Leon's risk and no one else's — and the upside was too good to pass up, pristine cards in Christian names from wiped-out towns up north.

When I brought the five identities to Marcel at his shop, his first reaction was, "There's no way. I can't do this many in two days. It isn't possible. You never said—"

I stopped him and explained that there was no rush on this bunch, that two weeks would be fine. But after that, I said, we would be back on, hopefully, a two-day turnaround schedule with two or three identities.

"How often again?" he said.

"I would say once a month, probably. Could be once every three weeks, but I think that would be stretching it. Once a month, two or three names, two-day turnaround."

Marcel bleated some more — he was genetically predisposed to dickering, it seemed — and we agreed on a price. I even agreed to pay the rush price for the packet of five identities I left him with even though there was no rush this time. Then, as part of the cover, I bought a 1907 postage stamp with the admonition, "Get some cheaper inventory in here — you're fucking me coming and going."

"Just another satisfied customer," Marcel said. We both laughed, and then I walked out of the shop and said a little prayer that there wasn't a Gestapo car waiting for me at the corner.

And with that, I attempted to live my normal life for the next two weeks, as Leon had instructed. Of course, seeing as how my day job was planning demolition events, normal had become a relative term. The next target had been selected for me, which I hated — a telephone exchange near Bron, about two miles past the eastern boundary of Lyon, maybe five miles from my house. But the research was the same — surreptitiously visiting at least three times, at different times of day, on different days of the week, dressed in a different get-up: business suit, farm laborer's clothing, and my new favorite, a priest's cassock.

As I worked out the details — and while the grand high council of Resistance assholes could pick the targets, they couldn't rush the planning, and I wouldn't be rushed — I had the vague sense that I was sometimes being followed. I could never prove it. The evasion tactics I employed — buses taken in the wrong direction, getting off trains at the last second and then doubling back, everything — never left me in a position to identify somebody who was definitely following me. Still, I just had a feeling. It was likely paranoia but, then again, if I didn't have a right to be paranoid, who did?

It was after a day of reconnaissance at the site when I decided to stop by the flat for a quick shower. It was when I unlocked the door that I saw Leon, a tiny woman and two tinier children, two boys, five-year-old twins. He was giving them a tour of the place, as much as that was necessary.

"... and this is our host, Alex," Leon said. "Alex, this is Myrna and her two children, Jean and Michel."

I screwed up a face at the two Christian names, which was rude but, what the hell. Leon laughed. So did Myrna. She said, "We are not that observant — like our friend here."

I had often said that Leon was the least Jewish Jew I had ever met. Back in Vienna, his girlfriends were almost exclusively Christians, as were about 90 percent of his friends — and he once proclaimed the pork tenderloin with a bitter cherry sauce at Horner's to be "exquisite." Of course, Adolf's boys didn't care about your denomination, or how often you went to shul. They just cared if your grandparents were Jewish. They started asking there, and then they loaded you into the train cars if they didn't like the answers.

"Where is your husband, if I may ask?"

Leon started to answer but Myrna jumped right in. Her voice was even, unemotional.

"We don't know," she said. "We haven't known for eight months. He worked as a tailor. His shop, a whole block of shops in the Marais, they were raided by the Gestapo late one after-noon. And we just don't know."

The boys were racing in circles around the sofa. Myrna started to yell at them but now it was Leon's turn to interrupt.

"Let them," he said. "Let them have a little fun. Besides, they'll sleep better."

While they ran, Leon finished the tour, ending up with the re-filled food cupboard. Myrna gasped. I told them to eat their fill for the next couple of days while they had the chance. She did not appear as if she was going to have to be told a second time.

Outside, I told Leon that he was earlier than I had expected and I wasn't sure if Marcel would have the new identity cards ready. "I told him two weeks," I said. "That's not for—" I began counting on my fingers "—four days."

I told Leon to go check with Marcel in the morning and see where things stood. "It's all paid for," I said, and then I asked him how many were in the group after next.

"Three," he said, and I counted out the money.

"So pick up the three identity cards for Myrna and her kids, and the two for the next group. Like I said, they're all paid for. Then give him the photos and information for the group after that, with the money. But if you have to wait a couple of extra days, you have to wait. There's enough food for them, and Manon will be happy to have you."

"Where are you going to be?"

"My day job," I said. "I leave early in the morning. Hopefully be back day after tomorrow. I'll come by the flat when I'm back. If you're still there, you're still there — but don't wait."

We ran over a couple of other details, and then I turned to leave. "You coming?"

"I think I might stay here with them," Leon said.

I just looked at him.

"On the couch," he said.

I kept staring.

"Really," he said.

19

I was getting ready to leave and Manon was acting weird. Not crazy, not angry, not snippy, not secretive — just a little odd. It was as if we were suddenly uncomfortable with each other, and I didn't know why.

I was going to make the trip in my farm laborer clothes — reasonably fresh shirt, trousers that were clean but with the discoloration baked into them, stained forever, and dusty work boots. The plan was for me to walk to the outskirts of the city and pick up a train there, then overshoot my intended station by one, then walk back on the farm roads that criss-crossed the fields. They were grain fields out that way, mostly wheat. As best as I could tell from the map, I would be walking 12 miles altogether before I took a nap in the tiny orchard that seemingly sprung up out of nowhere and fell away almost as quickly. There might have been 30 trees there in total. And if anyone came upon me, they would see nothing but a laborer taking advantage of a shady spot to sleep.

As I was tying the right boot, the lace snapped. I muttered a quick "shit," and Manon's reply was quick and urgent: "What's wrong? What?"

"Just a shoelace," I said, holding up the broken piece.

"I'll get you a new one," she said.

"No, don't. Better if I just tie the pieces together and make do. It's what a worker would do."

"I guess," she said.

It was just... odd. I had been on literally a dozen of these sabotage missions before and Manon had never acted this way. She knew how carefully I planned things. She often participated in the planning. On one job, she noticed a hole in my logic when it came to the timing of Gestapo guard schedules at a depot and suggested a change — and she was right. It would have worked my way, too, but her change bought us a few extra minutes. She was smart, and she was committed to what we were doing. Of course, she hadn't been pregnant for most of my earlier jobs.

"What's wrong?" I said, finally.

"I don't know," she said. She wasn't hiding the fact that something was bothering her.

"Something I did?"

"No."

"Worried about the job? Because you shouldn't be. This one is safer than the last one—"

"It's not that," she said. "I know you're careful. I'm not worried about that more than any of the others. It's just—"

"The baby?"

"No," Manon said. "At least I don't think so. It's just that I think there's more Gestapo around than there were. Did I tell you I saw two of them in The Cove yesterday?"

The Cove was a cafe about four blocks from our home, which meant it was pretty far outside the normal Gestapo perimeter.

"And it was during the day, late morning," she said. "Just two monkeys in their black suits, enjoying a cup of coffee, chatting and laughing away. I have to be honest, I felt like fucking throwing up."

I put my arm around here. "Not from the morning sickness?"

"From the uniform sickness," she said.

She was right — there were more Gestapo in the city. It wasn't an overwhelming presence, or anything approaching that, but it was growing. You would still be unlucky to be caught after curfew in our neighborhood, but it wasn't a long shot anymore. And more men meant more investigators trying to turn more Frenchmen into sources, either through force or bribery. And more sources meant more danger for people doing the kind of work that we were doing.

"So is that it?" I said. "Uniforms got you spooked? Because we always knew—"

"Stop being rational."

"Kind of hard to stop at age 43."

"Try," she said.

"Really, what's wrong?"

She had no answer. She just got up and left the room. It had been kind of weird ever since my visit to Avenue Berthelot and then the meeting with the other Resistance leaders, but this was worse. I still didn't know what to think about why Barbie had questioned me so gently, and why the vibe at the Resistance meeting was so tense. As best as I could tell, Rene had not been heard from, and that was awful, but it wasn't as if he were the first member of the Resistance to be caught. I just didn't know, and I didn't know what to do about it, and now it was affecting my relationship with Manon. And, truthfully, that's all I really had in my life, and all I wanted — that and the baby.

I was committed to the Resistance but, truth be told, it was a distant second place. There were days when I wondered if we shouldn't just pack up and flee to America — and if it could be accomplished with the snap of my fingers, I think it might have happened by now. That is, assuming I could have drugged Manon into submission, because she was different. She was French, and she was committed either to kicking out the Nazis or dying while trying. As with most things, it was more of an intellectual opposition by me and a visceral, emotional hatred on her part.

But something was different now. I just didn't know. I tried to convince myself it was the baby, but I wasn't sure. As I was leaving, I expected a perfunctory kiss from Manon, based upon the tension in the house. Instead, I received not a kiss, but an extended hug. It might have lasted a minute. She really seemed as if she didn't want to let me go.

20

I took the train to Genas and walked west from there, backtracking. It was a couple of miles. I saw the little orchard a half-hour before I reached it, sprouting out of the wheat fields that had just been prepared for planting. It took only a few seconds for me to find the tree I had climbed the last time, the one that was easiest for a 43-year-old man to shinny up.

The telephone exchange was maybe a half-mile away, the next sprout out of the wheat fields. It was just a little concrete box, two stories tall, with a small parking lot in the back, space for maybe five cars. There was one vehicle when I began watching: a black Citroen. That was the Gestapo car, and there was the same single guard at the door.

I reached into my pocket and took out my binoculars for a closer look. They were actually Manon's binoculars, procured when she worked for French intelligence in Zurich. She hated the Swiss, but they were Swiss made and so perfect that even she had to concede that the Swiss were good at something. They fit in the palm of your hand but were shockingly powerful. It was how I could tell the guard was the same kid I had seen on my last recon.

When they told me the target was going to be a telephone exchange, I sneered. Then they outlined for me how the system worked, that if you imagined the phone system as a tree, each of the exchange buildings was the place where a new branch grew out of the trunk, or out of a bigger branch.

The ass-grabbing prick from *Liberation* was doing the explaining. "This one," he said, pointing at the map, at the exchange I was now viewing through Manon's binoculars. "This one is the base of the tree of the Lyon phone system. It's the trunk — well, one of them. All the lines from the east come through that building and then begin to branch out on the other side."

It was true. You could see from the telephone poles that one set of wires entered into the building from the east side and that a half-dozen spokes of wires exited on the west side.

"So if you knock out that building—"

"You knock out the city," the ass-grabber said. "Well, that's not true. What you knock out is all telephone traffic from the east into the city, which means all telephone traffic from Germany, for instance. And the added bonus is that the telegraph lines share the same poles as the telephone lines."

"How long will they be out?" I said.

"If you do it right, maybe two weeks. It won't be a crisis but it will be a major inconvenience."

"So if it's such a vital spot, why is there only one guard?" I said.

"Either they don't quite realize the importance, or they figure it's far enough out of town not to be a concern, or maybe they don't want to draw any undue attention to it. Maybe they figure that a big Gestapo presence would only bring us to it."

Whatever the reason, there was only the single kid guarding the building. He looked like he was about 23 years old, and beyond bored. He had brought a lunch with him in a sack, and when it was time, he just unbuttoned and pissed next to the Citroen in the little parking area. If it was like the other times, the shifts would be 12 hours long, with the change-over at 6 p.m. The last time, the night-time guard was sitting in his car by 8 p.m., helmet off.

The telephone operators worked eight-hour shifts: 8 a.m., 4 p.m and midnight. There were six of them — one, apparently, for each of the lines that exited the building on the east side. A call would come in and be routed along one of those six lines, where another operator in another telephone exchange building in Lyon would route it again, and where a third operator in your neighborhood would direct it to the phone in your home.

I watched through the binoculars until the 4 p.m. shift change, and it was as before — six operators out, six operators in, all women, all on foot and walking toward Bron. Then I climbed down from my perch, laid down and closed my eyes. My cohorts would not arrive for hours, each carrying a suitcase containing enough explosive power to take down the telephone exchange. Max would have one suitcase, and another Max would be the demolitions expert. I had never met him before the single planning meeting we had the previous week.

"Two fucking Max's? Really?" I said.

"It's a great name, Pops."

"For now, you're Little Max. It's the only way I can keep it straight."

"Fuck you, Pops."

Both of the Max's were dressed for work, but Little Max was a mess. His shirt had a memorable stain on the right front pocket, perhaps mustard. And the hem on his left pants leg had entirely succumbed to time and wear — that leg of the trousers was three inches longer than the other leg, cut roughly and unevenly and dragging a little bit beneath the heel of his boot.

"Nice," I said, pointing to the offending pants leg. "You'll never get laid at this rate."

"You see any fucking women around here, Pops?" he said.

The new Max seemed a little put off by our banter. I just looked at him and said, "Don't worry, he'll be motherfucking you, too, once he gets to know you a little better."

They both arrived at around 7 p.m., from different directions. The plan was simple enough. We would overtake the snoozing guard, enter the building, tell the operators to run, set the explosives on a timer, and be back in the orchard by the time it all went boom.

The key word in that description: overtake. We were likely going to have to kill the guard, and I was the one with the pistol. It's odd that the thought of killing him did not bother me, not for a second. I take that back — the logistics of the thing bothered me, and the concern about the noise. But the morality? There wasn't any morality. I had undoubtedly shot someone with my rifle in the first war, although never up close. This would be a shot from right under his snout, probably. I was still hoping to knock him out and tie him up, but I really wasn't that optimistic. And I was okay with the alternative. Before this had all begun, back before the Germans had marched into Austria in 1938, I had lived my adult life pretty much as a physical coward. I didn't fight, and I avoided confrontation. Now, I was more than fine with the notion that I would end up shooting this kid as he dozed in the front seat of his Citroen. It was just another item on the checklist.

When I thought back on it later, I could still see him startled, helmet off, then trying to pick up his rifle and having it impeded by the steering wheel as he attempted to lift it into aiming position. I never really saw his face as he was turned away and looking down at the rifle and the steering wheel when I arrived at the driver's side door. I ended up needing only one shot. Check.

The rest went as planned, except for one slight hitch. One of the operators said, "Shouldn't you hit us or something? Make it look like we resisted?"

I looked at the two Max's. No one knew what to do.

Finally I said, "No, just run. Tell the truth. We had a gun, we had bombs. If you tried to stop us, we would shoot you. If you tried to stay, you would be blown up. Always stick with the truth, and that is the truth. So get the fuck out of here."

"Wait, Pops," Little Max said. "How far is the nearest house where you could call for help?"

I looked at the operator who had become the de facto spokesperson.

"Maybe a mile," she said.

Little Max said, "Shouldn't they—"

"Yeah," I said. "That's a good idea. All of you head for that house. Don't run, but walk fast. It'll take you 15 minutes that way, give or take. That's plenty of time. Call the Gestapo from there and tell them. That'll protect you even more if they ask questions."

The operators all left. I said, "All right, Max." He had placed some of the explosives downstairs and run a wire up the steps behind him. The second and third charges, with some incendiary elements, were in the second suitcase. He placed one at the spot where the trunk line from the east entered the building, and the other on the massive console where the operators worked.

"Timers?" he said.

"I know we said 10 minutes but make it eight."

A couple of things could trip us up. One would have been a random patrol, but I had not seen one in the three nights I had been watching. A second would have been someone coming out to the facility to check why calls from the east weren't getting through. That would take more than 10 minutes, though. So eight minutes just added a touch more safety. A determined run would get us back to the orchard in enough time.

As it turned out, we were back with about 30 seconds to spare, panting and doubled-over. The explosion hurt your ears, even from a half-mile away. The ground shook a bit beneath our feet, beneath the trees. Then the fire followed, lighting the night. The fields glowed.

21

Little Max had brought a flask with him, and we all took a long pull of something that he insisted was not a homemade brew. When I made a face — it tasted like petrol filtered through a dirty sock — he said, "It's legit, Pops. It isn't going to blind you. Your failing eyesight is all about your fucking old age."

Then we were off in three separate directions. Because Little Max had been caught by the Gestapo while hiding in a field the last time, we decided that constant movement might make more sense this time. There were several small-to-medium towns in the area — Bron, Villeurbanne and Venissieux. None was more than a three-mile walk from the orchard. The plan was to travel in the dark, through fields as necessary, and then to hide within the shopping district in each of those towns, amid the trash cans in an alley or some such place. Then it would be breakfast in the first cafe that opened, followed by the short commute back into the center of Lyon — by train, or bus, or on foot. Just one in a crowd.

It was clear to me that the most dangerous part would be the initial walk. Yes, it would be dark — but it would be the time when our proximity to the explosion was the closest. Also, anyone out walking in the middle of the night would be automatically suspicious. And I did have to dive into a gully by the side of the road when I saw some headlights in the distance, but I was lucky. The road was winding at that point, and there were a few rolling hills, and I could see the lights well before any occupants of the vehicle could possibly focus on where I was walking. The car sped by me, without incident. I wasn't sure it was the Gestapo, but it likely was, seeing as how it was coming from Lyon, and anyway, so few people had access to petrol anymore.

But that was it. Other than disassembling the pistol as I walked and throwing the pieces, one by one, as far as I could into the fields, one piece every five minutes or so, nothing else resembling caution or a diversion was required. Once into the towns, I thought we would be fine. I indeed hid between a couple of trash barrels behind the Marigold Cafe in Venissieux. At 7, I dusted myself off, walked around to the front door and entered. There were three men already leaning on the zinc-topped bar, having coffee and a croissant. I decided to sit, and after I checked the remnants of my ration cards, to have an egg, coffee and a roll, mostly because I hadn't seen an egg in a store in about two months. I was almost shocked to see it on the menu.

"Eggs?" I said to the waiter. His smile matched mine.

"My cousin's farm," he said. "It is your lucky day. We receive a dozen once or twice a month. They'll be gone in three hours. Limit is one per person."

I never received my egg. I had just ordered it when two Gestapo men, a uniform and a black trench coat, walked into the cafe and literally picked me up by the back of my shirt collar and hauled me out to their car, where I was cuffed to a metal bar that had been bolted to the back of the front seat. No one in the cafe even looked up from their coffee.

Neither of my new black-clad friends said a word. Neither of them asked my name or explained the reason for my arrest. I went with my customary indignant query — "What the fuck?" — and was greeted with the back of the trench coat's hand to my jaw. Apparently, they spoke French, or at least knew that much. Or maybe the back of the hand had become the standard reply in Lyon in 1943. And that was it. We drove in silence from Venissieux to Montluc, where I was dumped into the same waiting area as the last time. Only now, the guards were Gestapo. As he handed me over, the black trench coat said "Herr Killy" by way of introduction to my new keeper.

That was beyond concerning. He knew my name without asking. He knew my name without searching me or inspecting my identification. He recognized my face and knew exactly where to look for me at the cafe. Only three people knew the escape plan, but they didn't know which cafe I would be in, seeing as how even I didn't know until I came upon it. It was as if the Gestapo was a fourth member of our sabotage group. But how was that possible?

Again, it had to be one of the Max's. They must have been caught quickly and talked. And seeing as how this was now twice, and only Little Max and I were involved with both operations, he had to be the source. Except I didn't believe it. He was a young shithead, but I never doubted his loyalty or his commitment. I could see him talking if tortured — anybody would, probably — but he hadn't been tortured. He had taken a punch to the head but was let go almost as quickly as I was. There was no way he was working for the Gestapo as a kind of double-agent. There was just no fucking way.

So, who? A new guard came out and said, "Killy, Allain?" I stood up. It was then that the one tiny good part of my predicament dawned on me because I had made the decision to carry the Allain Killy identity card on this mission. The reason to switch would have been if I had been arrested by the Gestapo in another city, because Allain Killy showing up on a Gestapo report in, say, Dijon would be the link they needed on Avenue Berthelot to mark me as a certified member of the Resistance whom they already suspected. But an arrest in Lyon, or the suburbs, would just bring me right back to Avenue Berthelot anyway, where Barbie and some guards already knew my face. A different identity would have just been a waste.

"Okay, sit," the guard said. "We're waiting for two more."

There were three of us, cuffed to the backs of three different metal benches. We sat for maybe an hour, maybe more, waiting. One guy called out after a while, saying he needed the bathroom. When no one answered he half-stood and half-kneeled, one foot on the floor and one knee on the bench, and somehow managed to get himself unbuttoned and unleashed with one hand cuffed to the railing, pissing against the wall. I offered him a silent bravo upon his completion.

When the next two prisoners finally arrived, I don't know if I was relieved or even more worried when neither of them was named Max.

22

I t was the same drill. Right at 9 o'clock again, the five of us were shackled into the back of an open lorry. None of us knew each other, so no one talked. It was the same fear, that a Gestapo informant had been planted among the group. And while there was a very human need to make contact with someone, to share the experience as a way of alleviating some of the terror of the unknown, simple common sense meant that the sharing would have to be in silence. The grinding of the lorry's gears, the whoosh of the wind, the noises of the city — those would fill in the gaps.

Again, we took the same stupid route. While the guards at Montluc had changed over to the Gestapo, the driver and the guard running the transport to Avenue Berthelot were French. I still couldn't tell if there was some security reason for going this way, or if it was just a time-wasting opportunity to prolong the minutes the French guards were out from under the Gestapo's noses. But it was the same odd lefts and the same strange rights, eventually taking us through the place with the sign that said "Fort La Motte." I still didn't know what it was. Without the military buildings, it could be a park.

It still made no sense. It should have been a 10-minute ride, tops, and that was if you got stuck behind one of those buses with the hybrid engines, running sometimes on petrol and sometimes on burning wood, the smoke belching out of what amounted to a furnace bolted onto the front of the engine. If the wind was wrong, I wondered how the driver could see, or how the passengers could breathe. Without the hindrance of a bus, the more direct route would have been five or six minutes. But we took more than 20 minutes, or at least it seemed that way.

It was all sickeningly the same as the last time, including the unloading process. We all had been unshackled from the lorry and jumped down into the courtyard at Avenue Berthelot when a uniform with a clipboard arrived and asked, "Killy, Alain?"

I stepped forward. As the lorry drove off, he shouted over the noise, "The rest of you will go with my colleagues here. Killy, you are to come with me." And from there, it was in through the familiar door, up the familiar flight of steps, and into the same chair in the same outer office, next to the same desk manned by the same factotum. I was waiting for Klaus Barbie, again.

As it turned out, he was already behind the closed door of the inner office. A buzz at the secretary's desk was the signal for me to enter. Barbie was seated at the desk, the lamp on. He was leaning over, straining to read what must have been some small print on a document he was holding up to his face. Hildy the German shepherd was snoozing on the rug behind the desk. It was all as I had left it.

"Sit, sit, Herr Killy," Barbie said, not looking up from the paper, just waving vaguely at the chair. "Or should I call you Herr Kovacs? Or perhaps, if you don't consider it too familiar, I should call you Pops?"

Whatever color remaining in my face at that point had almost certainly vanished. Pops. Shit. There were two possibilities. Maybe, or probably, they had Little Max and had forced him to talk — although I'm not sure he knew my real name. The other possibility was the group of telephone operators. It had dawned on me as I walked to Venissieux in the dark, replaying the operation in my head, that a mistake had been made. Little Max had called me Pops in the operators' presence. He had said "Wait, Pops," before asking the women where the nearest house was. They had undoubtedly been questioned by the Gestapo in the hours after the explosion, and one of them had likely offered up this tidbit — Pops — as a way to please the interrogators.

The more I thought about it, the more sense that made. Where the name Kovacs had come from, though, was the mystery. I hadn't used it on an official document in nearly two years. One of our friends might have slipped up and said Alex instead of Allain, but almost nobody knew Kovacs.

Not that it mattered, though. I was sitting in Barbie's office again, wearing handcuffs again. Whatever the name, he had me.

After several uncomfortable minutes — although I'm not sure what a comfortable minute in Barbie's presence might have felt like — he put down the paperwork and snapped off the switch on the desk lamp.

"Where were you last night, Allain Killy?" he said.

"Home with my wife."

"And why the cafe in Venissieux? It's a long way from home."

"Eggs," I said.

"Excuse me?"

"Two days a month, they have eggs on the menu. I was craving one."

"Cooked how?"

"Poached."

"Hard or runny?"

"Runny is the only way," I said. "With a baguette to mop up the yolk."

"And did you get your egg this morning?"

"No, I was interrupted."

"A pity," Barbie said.

He stood up. The dog did too, with a growl. "Now, now, Hildy, you remember our friend here. Mind your manners."

Barbie motioned for me to walk ahead of him. We left the inner office, and then the outer office, and headed into a stairwell at the end of the hallway. We walked up to the fourth floor and, when we arrived, Barbie moved in front of me and opened a heavy fire door.

23

There were no offices on this part of the fourth floor. There were no walls. It was a big, open space with unfinished floors and industrial lighting fixtures. It had likely been used for storage at one point. That was no longer the case, though.

There were no other people there, only Barbie and I — and Hildy, let off her leash to run around and sniff and growl.

"Come, come," Barbie said. "I must give you the tour."

It was a torture chamber. There was no other way to describe it. I sensed it as soon as we entered and knew it for sure as we approached the various stations, all equipped for horror.

"Have you noticed?" Barbie said, patting the wall as we walked. "Such beautiful stone walls. So strong. So thick. With only a couple of windows up here, all at the far end, you can't hear a thing outside." He stopped and patted the wall again. "So, so thick," he said.

Our first stop was a gas stove that was blazing even with nobody up here. The warmth it gave off felt good, almost comforting. Sticking out of the opening were a half-dozen metal rods with wooden handles. They looked like the pokers you would use to tend a wood fire in a fireplace. That they had a different use in the hands of the Gestapo was soon more than clear.

Barbie removed one of the pokers from the stove. He held it up, admiring it. The iron glowed red.

"Do you know," he said, "that the very sight of this simple implement is enough to get a man to answer a question he might otherwise prefer to skip over, or to entice him to recall a detail that he thought he had forgotten. Sometimes all you need to do is to hold it, red and hot like this, up to the man's face. Not even to touch the skin. Just to hold it at eye level."

He did that to me. I did everything I could not to move.

"Turn around," Barbie said, and I did. He lowered the poker and held it against my ass. I could smell my trousers burning, and then my underwear, and then my skin. The whole thing didn't take 15 seconds before he removed it. I would undoubtedly have a scar, but I doubted there was any permanent damage. Ass fat would likely grow back.

He had not yet asked me a question beyond the initial couple in his office. But after he had put the poker back into the stove, he merely motioned for me to follow him to the next station on the hellish assembly line. It consisted of an examining table, like you might see in a doctor's office, but with leather restraints for the hands and the feet.

I began to hoist myself on the table, but Barbie said, "No, no. Just look. And over there," he said, pointing at the wall opposite the foot of the table. There were tools hanging on a pegboard as if it were the side wall of a farmer's barn. There were two small saws and a half-dozen cutters, the kind you might use to prune bushes, from fine hand nippers to a great set of loppers that would cut a three-inch tree branch.

He reached for the loppers, examined them up close, and shook his head. "Such sloppiness," he said, and wiped something from the crux of the two blades with a nearby rag. He showed me what was on the rag, and while I couldn't tell for sure, it appeared to be a combination of blood and tissue.

I could barely breathe at that point, but I continue to look around. I didn't see my greatest fear, which was electric wires that could be attached to my balls. I didn't doubt that they had them, but I didn't see them.

"Come along now," Barbie said, and we walked to the far corner of the vast space. There were two battleship-sized bathtubs, side by side. There also was another gas stove with enormous pots, presumably to boil water. Then, next to them, was the last of a melting block of ice.

"Look, look up," Barbie said, pointing to the space above the bathtubs. There was a pulley contraption bolted to the ceiling, with a thick rope attached to one wall. On the other end of the rope, a long metal bar was attached at both ends. The bar had two cross-pieces attached about three or so feet apart.

I looked a little quizzically and Barbie said, "Imagine being stripped naked. Now imagine being tied to the metal bar, trussed up, your arms attached to the one crossbar and your feet attached to the other.

"Now," he said, and Barbie grew even more enthusiastic here. His tone until then had been that of a proud homeowner showing off his new paint job. But this was different. I had been afraid of him the whole time, and more afraid when he burned my ass with the poker, but this was a different level entirely.

"Now," he said, "imagine one of these tubs filled with boiling water and the other filled with ice water. Now imagine, trussed onto the bar, being lifted up by the pulley and then lowered into the boiling water. You don't drown — you can't drown, because the crossbar catches on the sides of the tub and prevents you from being lowered too far — but you are completely beneath the water level. Your face might be covered for a short time. And then you are lifted out of the boiling water, hoisted up on the pulley and then lowered into the ice water."

He stopped and closed his eyes. It was as if Barbie was replaying the vision in his head.

"Boiling and freezing is usually enough," he said. "We usually don't even have to dunk him into the boiling water a second time to get what we need."

He looked at me as if he was expecting me to say something. But I had nothing. I mean, nothing. And Barbie seemed somewhere between annoyed and disappointed.

"Okay, the tour is over, Herr Killy," he said. "Come, come — but be careful. Don't trip on those things. This place is a pig sty. My men will hear from me about this."

I turned without looking and barely avoided what Barbie had been indicating. It was a pair of trousers, laid haphazardly on the floor. What caught my eye was the hem on one of the pants legs, and how it was completely undone, about three inches of extra pants, the bottoms roughly and unevenly cut, worn out in one place, as if it had been trailing beneath the back heel of a pair of work boots.

I threw up where I stood, then leaned over and retched some more. Hildy ran over and fussily sniffed my vomit, then backed away.

"This way, Pops," Barbie said.

He walked me down to his office and handed me off to the secretary without comment or even a glance in my direction. The secretary called for a guard to walk me back down to the courtyard. There, though, instead of waiting for another trip on a lorry back to Montluc, the clipboard came over and said, "You are free to go, Herr Killy." He pointed me toward the front gate.

Free to go? What the hell?

As I walked, I began to feel the burn on my ass a little more — I guess the remaining fabric was irritating it as I moved with each step. But it was only an irritation. For the second time, I was being allowed to leave — and this time, I didn't even have to go back to Montluc. And then there was Max. God, those pants. He was a tough little fucker, but it was hard to imagine surviving some of those tortures. I wanted to hang around in the courtyard and see if he was brought out for the ride back to Montluc, but the clipboard was having none of it. He rushed me along and watched me as I walked.

I don't know if he saw me look up at one of the second-floor windows near the gate. The person who stood there and watched me from behind the window was maybe 20 feet away, glowering down. He stared at me, and I stared at him. He didn't react, and I didn't react. He didn't lower his eyes or look away, and I finally did. I couldn't believe it, and I would have thrown up again if I thought I had any ammunition left.

As I was going through the gate, I took one more look over my shoulder to be sure. Unfortunately, I was. Standing there, still staring, was Werner Vogl.

24

It was in Cologne, in the days before the Anschluss, when I hatched the plot to kill Werner Vogl. After an adult life that was the opposite of audacious, my plan was to murder a Gestapo captain on German soil as revenge for the role he played in killing my Uncle Otto.

Leon, whose life was defined by its audacity, thought I was crazy — although he did acknowledge that the plan wasn't half-bad. Vogl was an odd one. He was trying to catch a spy, an Abwehr general who happened to be an old friend of my uncle. Because of the family connection, he suspected me of espionage, too — but when he wasn't trying to scare me, he was showing off to me. Vogl was a Nazi pseudo-intellectual, and couldn't understand why the occasional application of electric wires to the gonads wasn't seen as a good thing by the citizens of the Reich.

He could quote from Nazi tracts. He made elaborate comparisons to the Roman empire. When he wasn't doing that, he was showing off his own little jail, in the basement of his headquarters building in Cologne. He allowed the prisoners to write on the walls and he allowed their words — some hopeful, some despairing — to remain for the next poor saps to see.

It was as if he was showing off his place in history when he gave me the tour of the cells. And because he talked to me, I learned a couple of his fastidious habits. I knew the bar where he drank and played chess on Tuesday nights, and I knew the place where he always parked his big black Gestapo Daimler, and I knew the alley he walked through to get from the bar to his car. I was waiting for him in the alley one night with a knife that had belonged to Otto, a bad-movie cliche. And I would have killed Vogl, too, if the Abwehr general had not intervened with the police at the last second, setting me up as the patsy in a plot to frame Vogl as the traitor. And while anyone who knew Vogl would have thought it was absurd — he was the straightest of arrows, a Nazi true believer to an absurd level — the frame-up worked just fine. Vogl ended up being arrested, and I was shipped back to Austria, just in time for the German invasion.

The last time I had seen him was back then, in 1938, when he was being led away and presumably booked for passage to Dachau. The last time I had heard his name was in 1940 when a man I trusted from Swiss intelligence told me that Vogl had made inquiries about me to the German consulate in Zurich. He said that Vogl was attached to a Gestapo unit in Warsaw — that's where the telegram to Zurich had originated. It scared the shit out of me that he wasn't in jail, that he had somehow rehabilitated his reputation with his bosses, but I was out of Zurich within days and I hadn't heard his name since.

But now it was 1943 and there he was, staring down from that window on Avenue Berthelot. There was no doubt that it was him, and there was no doubt that he had seen me. Suddenly, it made perfect sense that Barbie had known my real name. But that was the only thing that made perfect sense. The rest was a fog — and any hope I might have had of working my way out of it had vanished when the sight of Vogl left me feeling concussed.

I walked in circles for hours. I didn't see anyone following me, but I didn't trust anybody anymore, least of all myself. I once thought I was good at this, and it wasn't that long ago. It was hours ago, actually. I had always felt the adrenaline rush of espionage, and while I hated it when spies or Resistance fighters referred to it as "the game," I understood it because I had felt it. I still felt it. The urgency of running back to the orchard, the elation when the bombs exploded, the camaraderie with the two Max's — there was no doubt that it was a rush, and that it was a feeling that my body had begun to crave.

I was good at it. I was making a difference. That was what I'd felt not 12 hours earlier — and I was going to get to eat an egg besides. Now everything was in question, all of it. Because for the second time, my sabotage crew had been betrayed — either by Max, or someone else, or by my sloppiness. And now the Gestapo was, well, they were just fucking with me, arresting me and then releasing me back into the world. It was as if they believed I was doing them more good on the outside than in a cell at Montluc. And maybe I was. Maybe I was an amateur after all. Except that made no sense, either. I mean, the little stone bridge and the telephone exchange building, both lying in rubble, were a testament to something. If I were such an incompetent why didn't they stop me before the bombs went boom?

My mind raced from anecdote to anecdote, from scene to scene — but the fog and the fear were preventing me from making any connections between them and constructing a narrative that made sense. From scene to scene. On one of our little jobs a few months earlier, I'd asked Max an apparently absurd question as he removed some explosives from a box. They were perfectly safe to handle without the detonator attached, which I knew but forgot. Anyway, Max looked at me as if I were 85 years old and addled, and he said, "Don't be a dumb fuck, Pops." And, well, maybe I was a dumb fuck — a dumb fuck who was now in Werner Vogl's sights.

It took me eight hours to walk home. I sat on a park bench for an hour along the way. I nursed a cup of fake coffee in a cafe for another hour. And circles — I just walked in circles. I wouldn't have gone home at all if the Gestapo didn't already know the address, if they hadn't already arrested me there and searched the place and questioned Manon. Still, I was afraid to go there. I was afraid to go anywhere.

25

It was about 10 p.m. when I walked in the front door. Manon was still awake, reading a newspaper. The headline was something about a great victory in Kiev. My immediate assumption was that it was bullshit, unless it wasn't. With the newspapers, you couldn't know anymore. I believed that the Germans had double-crossed the Russians and invaded back in 1941, but I had no idea about the rest of it. The German could all be dead in Kiev or they could be knocking on doors in Vladivostok, and there was no way to tell for sure. When we heard it, the BBC said the Germans were struggling, and I hoped it was true, but I really didn't believe anybody about anything anymore.

Manon leaped up from her chair and greeted me with a hug, another long and silent hug. Neither of us spoke, not a word, as she led me by the hand into the bedroom and began undoing the buttons of my shirt. When I turned around, she saw my seared buttock for the first time. She began to say something, to ask, and I said, "Later." We made love then, me only on top to protect my ass as best as I could. When we were done, she got something to disinfect it and a bandage to cover it. It only stung for a few seconds.

"Well," she said, finally, after screwing the cap back on the bottle of the stinging stuff. And then I told her. I started with, "The good news is, we blew the shit out of the telephone exchange building," and then I told her the rest, all of it.

I went through everything — the guard I shot, the walk in the dark afterward, and the pistol that I disassembled and heaved into the fields, piece by piece. Then I told her about the cafe that I hid behind, and the eggs on the menu, and the silent arrest by the Gestapo. Then I told her about the wait at Montluc, and the lorry ride over to Avenue Berthelot, and the tour of the torture space on the fourth floor, the tour with Klaus Barbie as my guide. And then, when I told her about nearly tripping over the pants on the floor, the pants with the hem that had given way on one leg, I broke down and cried and couldn't continue. I was crawled up in a ball on the bed and the sobbing took over my body.

Manon had been silent throughout my recitation, silent and unable to wipe the worry from her face. She held me as my body heaved, and she said, "Alex, I'm so, so sor—"

"But that might not be the worst of it," I said.

And then I told her about being set free so quickly, and about staring down Werner Vogl as he stood in that window. I had told her the Vogl story exactly once, years before, but she apparently needed no refresher course on the subject. She seemed to recognize his name right away, and the implications, because then Manon was the one who was crying, a single tear falling down her cheek.

I leaned over and licked the tear away, attempting to break the mood and make her laugh. I succeeded for maybe a nanosecond. Her face grew even darker.

"Is there something else?" I said. "I mean, other than what I just said? Is there something bad you're not telling me? Is it the baby?"

"No, no, your son or daughter is fine," Manon said. "But you're right."

"What is it?"

She didn't answer.

"What? You have to tell me."

"I agree," she said. And then she told me "Maurice left here maybe 10 minutes before you walked in."

Maurice Peter was the head of another small resistance group, like ours. Behind his back, Manon and I made fun of how half-assed their newspaper was, and we thought the name — *Blue Sky* — was ludicrous. But within the council of Resistance groups, Maurice was our friend, always loyal. For all we knew, he made fun of our half-assed group behind our backs, too.

"So, what?" I said.

"Maurice came to tell me that there was an emergency meeting of the Resistance council at 6 p.m.," Manon said.

"Why didn't you go?"

"I wasn't invited."

"What does that mean?" I said. "How could you not have been invited?"

Manon explained that Maurice was coming by to tell her as a favor. He said that the reason the meeting was called was the news of our arrests in the morning.

"He said that you were seen being taken into Montluc," Manon said.

"Me, or all three of us?"

"That wasn't clear," she said. "He just said 'you,' and I don't know if he meant all of you. But the council is worried that the arrests are happening more frequently, and that they're happening so quickly."

Her voice trailed off.

"And?" I said.

She paused before answering. It was as if she were screwing up her courage.

"Just fucking say it," I said.

"They're worried the Gestapo has a spy within the council. And after you were spotted leaving Avenue Berthelot, they're becoming convinced that the spy is you. That's why I wasn't invited to the meeting. And that's why Maurice was taking a big chance by telling me."

So there it was. What had been a hint weeks earlier was now being stated as a fact. The guy with the Alsatian accent and all of the money was now officially suspected of betraying his wife and the Resistance movement. Alex Kovacs, Allain Killy, a Czech who lived most of his life in Vienna, a salesman for the family mining business, a bank president in Zurich, a spy against the Germans, an accomplished saboteur, an unthinking fucking assassin of a German kid guarding a telephone exchange building, was really a rat. That's what they believed.

We laid in bed, quiet again. Manon fell asleep within minutes. I didn't, and tossing and turning wasn't much of an option, given my sore ass. It was difficult enough to find a comfortable position as it was, but my ass and the endless racing of my mind made it both physically and mentally impossible to sleep. After I don't know how long, I got out of bed and went into the living room. Manon never stirred.

26

T he truth was, I did understand why the rest of the council figured me for a spy. I was furious that they didn't trust me, and hurt that all I had done for them was being discarded so easily, but I got it. I saw the arrests increasing and happening so quickly. I saw how I had been let go by the Gestapo not once, but twice — and with nothing more than a burn mark on my rump. It absolutely looked bad. It was a circumstantial case, but I did recognize that this was a hell of a set of circumstances.

Everybody's blood was up, too. The arrival of the Gestapo in town had added so much tension (the polite word in Resistance circles), so much fear (the real truth). At the beginning, we were fighting against the Vichy lunkheads and, while it wasn't easy, the danger was more manageable. This was another level of fear entirely, and it was getting worse as more and more men in black uniforms arrived in Lyon.

So many Resistance fighters had been picked up and questioned in the last few weeks and months. We all knew what the worst-case scenario was — that, after losing a finger or a toe, someone on our side would become a Gestapo informant in exchange for keeping the rest of his digits. We all liked to think that we would let them kill us before turning against the Resistance, that we would insist on them killing us, but none of us really knew. The truth was, I might throw up the next time I walked into that torture chamber, the second I walked through the threshold, before anyone had even begun to run the bath water. The terror was real in the abstract, and it was even worse in the reality.

Everyone was excited, on edge, afraid, and it would only get worse if Max or Little Max turned up dead. And there I was, walking out of Avenue Berthelot and into the sunshine. I got it. But it left me in a position where, outside of Manon, I didn't know who I could trust. Because the council didn't trust me, and Barbie really was just fucking with me, and then there was Vogl, staring down from that window. So, as far as trusted associates, I had Manon, and I had Leon — although, for all I knew, he had already picked up the identity cards and gotten on the train with Myrna, the little lady, and her two little kids.

The more I thought about it, though, the more I became convinced that involving Manon and Leon any more than necessary was unfair to both of them. They might be able to help — especially Manon — but the risk/reward calculation was so far out of whack as to be incalculable. They both would give me shit for my risk/reward tendencies — more than anybody in my life, ever, they were the two who acted most on instinct and decried my caution — but I couldn't help it. And the risks here were not only increasing, they were coming from several directions. They were coming from so many directions that I still couldn't even get a handle on them.

I needed time to think. I needed the safety of anonymity. Most of all, I needed to fucking calm down— and I could never calm down if I knew I was adding to the risk surrounding Manon. If I couldn't protect her, at least I could avoid exposing her to more danger. And the best way to do that was to go away, at least for a while.

So I grabbed a second set of clothes from the closet, careful not to wake her, and she did not stir. I stuffed the clothes into a small canvas knapsack, not much bigger than what a worker might carry to bring his lunch to a job site.

And then I wrote this note:

M y love,

    Hopefully, I have been gone for hours as you read this. You were sleeping so peacefully, and I hope I did not disturb you. Never forget that you are sleeping for two now. No matter how desperate things become, never forget that — or how much I love you. You are my life.

    The more I have thought about it, the more it seemed important that I disappear for a while. There is so much about the current situation that I don't understand, but it is becoming clearer and clearer that I am in danger. I get it but I don't get it — and that's why I am so concerned. If I understood what was going on, I could work to protect myself and to protect you. But I don't understand, and that just heightens the risk, and I cannot allow that risk to touch you or the baby in unnecessary ways.

    So I am gone for now. Please try not to worry. Even in my current fog, I am reasonably competent at what I do for a living. A good night's sleep or two will hopefully clear that fog, at least some of it, and then I will have a better idea how to proceed. But in the meantime, that means I need to be away from you.

    On the one hand, this might be stupid — because of how much I value your opinion and your insight. You are likely reading this and thinking I am an idiot for abandoning that insight and wisdom, and you could be right. But I hope you can see it from my perspective. I could not live with myself if my proximity to you resulted in something bad happening to you. I know what I signed up for, and I know what you signed up for, and danger was clearly part of it. But this has spiraled into something else, something beyond the control of both of us. The risks have grown significantly in the last day. I cannot expose you to those risks if I can avoid it.

So I am gone. Please don't try to find me — because while you're good, you're not that good (if I do say so myself). It's best for now that you do not know where I am. If it pains you to be apart half as much as it pains me, this will be difficult — but it is for the best. In your heart, I hope you can see that.

Please be reassured that this is only for a little while — maybe days, maybe weeks, hopefully not much more. But however long it is, just know that I will be back. You left me in Zurich once and I came to find you, and you should know that whatever happens, I will always come to find you.

Make sure to burn this when you are done reading it. And also get rid of the clothes I left behind. It will make for a better story if the Gestapo does come calling — that I left nothing behind, and that you assume I've gone for good, and that you have no idea where. Hopefully you will start showing soon, so that if they do come to question you, well, you know.

There is enough money in the account to last you indefinitely, and some in the box buried behind the house besides. Now burn this before you forget. And know that I will be back. Even in my current fog, I know that is a promise that I shall keep.

A

27

As it was after the curfew, I hid out in one of the traboules until sunrise. It was the one at 55 Rue de Tables Claudiennes. The residents sometimes locked the doors at night, but I pushed this one and it opened. Deep in the courtyard, there was a dark corner. It was a dry night, and not very cold, and I actually managed to fall asleep for a while, my head propped up on my knapsack.

The noise of doors slamming and men leaving for work were what woke me. Some undoubtedly saw me, sleeping in the common area beneath their homes. If it had been 1730, or 1830, or 1930, one of them would have rousted me and kicked my ass out of the traboule and onto the street because, truth be told, I did look like a bum. My clothes were not exactly my best — those were left behind in the house. I hadn't shaved in two days. My hair was no doubt wild — and it needed to be cut besides.

But it wasn't 1730, or 1830, or 1930. It was 1943, and the Gestapo were running Lyon, and no one tossed me out. Several of the men just looked away after seeing me. Two offered a thumbs-up and a mouthed "vive la France." Then a man brought me a cup of fake coffee and three or four inches of a stale-ish baguette. "Sorry, it's all we can spare," he said. He pointed to a nearby window sill and told me to leave the empty cup there.

For a minute or so, I was filled with hope. But then I thought about the men who wouldn't look me in the eye and decided that I needed to be moving, quickly, just in case. Because for all of the brave men and women of the Resistance, and all of the rest who were silently cheering us on, like the man with the coffee and the baguette, there were traitors, too. And there were those silently watching and deciding that maybe there would be a small advantage to be had by turning in the bum sleeping in their traboule.

It was what the Germans had robbed us of when they arrived — trust. The truth was that you just didn't know who you could trust, who you could believe. My list consisted of Manon and Leon, and that was it. For everybody else, you were always trying to calculate the angles they might be playing or the stresses they were under, or the threats. You just didn't know. I just didn't know.

My goal for the morning was to find another flat. I had more than enough money to leave the advanced month's rent that would be required. I also had the third identity card with me. Goodbye, Allain Killy. Hello, Albert Kampe. Even though that was the oldest of my fake identities, it remained pristine — mostly because I had only used it before the Gestapo came to Lyon, and also because I had never applied for a ration card with it.

So, as I walked south, I repeated it again and again like a mantra — Albert Kampe, Albert Kampe, Albert Kampe. Three or four miles from our Croix-Rousse neighborhood was Saint-Fons. It was near Venissieux, where I had been caught in the cafe, but it was a distinct neighborhood known mostly for one thing: Jews.

I had considered how much sense that either did or did not make. Saint-Fons was one of Lyon's main Jewish neighborhoods, and part of me figured that it was an area where the Gestapo paid extra attention. So that was a downside. But because it was an outlying neighborhood, my concern likely was a bit over-stated. And because it was a Jewish neighborhood, it probably possessed in abundance what I needed most: a vacant flat.

After the German invasion, Jews flocked to Lyon. Well, not exactly flocked. There weren't that many Jews in the city, maybe 1,000 or 1,500 families. Even if that number doubled, it was only a tiny sliver of the population. But since the Gestapo got here, the Jews had fled further south, and the ones that didn't leave quickly enough were being scooped up by the Gestapo in increasing numbers. That meant empty flats and increasingly desperate landlords who might not be that picky. And so it was. As I made the walk down Avenue Diderot, the "FOR RENT" signs sprouted like sunflowers.

I walked up and down the street and picked out the shittiest building of the bunch. It was likely a brown stone building, or maybe gray stone — except that the soot on the outside was thick enough to write your name with your finger. The tempta-tion was to think that a good sandblasting would take care of it and restore a bit of attractiveness. But the more I thought about it, the soot might have been the only thing that was holding the place together.

I knocked at the door of the superintendent which was a few steps below street level — and let's just say that she fit the place perfectly. He hair was a henna'd nest. Her housecoat had a magnificent stain on her left breast — or, rather, where her left breast had resided several decades previously. She grabbed a ring of keys and walked me inside.

"I have three one-bedrooms — you want the front or the back?" she said.

"Back," I said.

"Just you?"

"Just me. They're furnished, right?"

She eyed me up.

"I have one with a bed, a set of drawers and a couch," she said.

"That should be fine."

She unlocked the door. It was even more of a shithole than I anticipated — and my expectations were pretty much subterranean. I must have made a face, to which my soon-to-be-landlady responded with indignation.

"Keep your goddamn face to yourself," she said. "I'm not asking you any questions. I'm not asking you why a man with a wedding ring needs a furnished apartment. So I'll get you a mop and a bucket and a clean set of sheets, and you'll give me a month's rent in advance, and we'll get along fine. Won't we?"

I peeled off the money and she crammed it into her bosom. She pulled a lease out of her pocket, wrote Albert Kampe on it, and barely glanced at my identity card. After I signed, she brought the mop and the bucket and the sheets. I scrubbed until I wasn't afraid to sit on the toilet anymore. After about two hours, the shithole had been transformed into a gleaming shithole. It would do.

And then I walked. I wasn't sure of anything, other than that I had not been followed to Saint-Fons. Leaving the apartment, I circled and doubled back enough that I was still pretty sure I was okay. So then I just walked and tried to come up with a plan. I wasn't paying that much attention to where I was. I wanted to stop by the other flat to see if Leon and the Jews were gone, but I would wait until dark for that. In the meantime, I was just wandering. I ended up near old Lyon, and even though I had overshot it, I decided to backtrack and climb the hill to the Roman ruins, partly to burn off some nervous energy but mostly because the funicular kind of scared me. The idea of being cooped up in any enclosed place, even for just a few minutes, scared me.

So I walked up Montee Saint-Barthelemay, taking my time up the half-mile hill, stopping in doorways occasionally to look back. There was nobody following me, not that I could see, but my paranoia was intense. God, I needed a night's sleep. By the time I reached the ruins, it was getting near sunset. I sat there in the amphitheater and tried to figure out what to do. I was in the top row, and it was quite a scene, even only half-excavated — the rows of stone seats, the shadows falling on the great stage, and the sun dipping behind the city when I looked back over my right shoulder.

After a few minutes, it was nearly dark. And in the gloaming, I could not see the shooter but I heard the rifle shots. One. Two. The first hit nothing. The second hit the row in front of me. Something hit my hand — it wasn't a bullet, just a stinging spray of stone chips. I scrambled back over the top row and lay down and hid behind it. The shooting stopped as quickly as it began.

28

I needed to walk east, but I walked west. I needed to hide, but I had nowhere to hide. I needed to calm down, to figure this out, but I had no idea how. And so I trudged in the dark of a darkened city, clueless.

I needed to get to the flat and talk to Leon, which was east of the Roman ruins. That is, if Leon was still there. Either way, I had to find out. But instead of going east, I went west and then south and then, finally, east. I kept checking for a tail as I took the great circle route even though whatever confidence I'd had in my abilities to spot a tail had disappeared in an instant. Two shots, one, two. An instant. Why did I even pretend I had a fucking chance to survive this?

A half-mile or so from the flat, I heard squealing tires and then slamming car doors as I approached an intersection. I pressed myself against the side of the last building and peered around the corner. It was completely dark at that point, and I was in a shadow besides, so I was reasonably confident as I watched. And it was still two hours before the curfew, so I technically wasn't doing anything wrong.

What unfolded was a scene that I had first witnessed years earlier in Cologne. It was in a different country and more than five years later, but it was the same chilling dynamic. The big black car pulled up — a Daimler back then, a Citroen now — and the black uniforms came out and beat on the apartment door. When it was opened, the uniforms rushed passed whoever opened it and inside. Minutes later, they returned with a half-dressed man, one holding each arm. The poor sap was unsuccessfully trying to squirm away. A woman suddenly appeared and began wailing. The third man in black — a trench coat, not a uniform — raised his hand to the woman and she at least reduced the volume of her crying. After the prisoner was secured in the back seat of the Citroen, the trench coat left the woman on the front steps and got into the front passenger seat. Then, with another squeal, the car rocketed out of the parking spot as quickly as it arrived. And as the woman began wailing louder again, I looked up at the apartment windows nearby. There were faces peering out from behind the curtains, 10 faces, 20 faces, more. It was just like Cologne.

That's when it hit me. It wasn't the Gestapo that had taken the shots at me in the amphitheater. It was the Resistance.

It was suddenly so clear — and it should have been all along. The Gestapo did not do long-distance rifle shots. They did terror. They pulled men away from their crying wives. They cut off your fingers and zapped your balls with electric current. They broke you down, and then they watched you die. A rifle shot from a couple of hundred yards away would be, for them, a dry hump. Where was the satisfaction in that?

No, it was the Resistance. Maybe someone followed me all day, but I really didn't think so. Maybe I was just unlucky, and somebody spotted me on the street. That was likely it. But whatever the mechanics, it was clear at that point that they didn't trust me anymore. They thought I was a Gestapo informant, and that I had to go. Fuck Manon, fuck everything I had done for them — I just had to go. One. Two.

29

The only thing I felt good about was leaving Manon and our home. I could not imagine how she would react to what had just happened. Actually, I could. She would be furious. She would get in the face of whoever in the Resistance would listen. She also might get herself shot in the process. The truth was, the closer I was to her, the greater the danger. Maybe this way they would believe that whatever they thought about me, Manon was still loyal to the cause.

The truth also was that Leon had to understand how much more dangerous his already-insanely dangerous enterprise had become. It was the only reason I was going back to the flat — and, for better or worse, Leon was still there with Myrna and the two kids.

"Marcel said he would have the identity cards in the morning," Leon said. "We have tickets on the noon train. It should be all good."

"Look, I have some things to tell you and not a lot of time." I stopped and looked at Myrna. "Just me and him, okay?"

She nodded darkly and returned to the kitchen where the children were eating.

When she was out of earshot, I told Leon everything that happened in the prior 48 hours, from the sabotage in Bron to the rifle shots in the amphitheater. He mostly listened until I got to the part about Vogl.

"Holy fuck — that guy?" Leon said.

"One and the same."

"Holy fuck. Holy fuck. My God, what are the odds?"

"It's no accident," I said. "We both know that."

"You think he can get himself transferred to wherever he wants?"

"Maybe you're right," I said. "But he found me in Zurich, and now he's found me here, and I'm starting to think that, yes, maybe he got himself transferred here somehow to settle up accounts."

When I got done everything — including describing the little Gestapo dance I had witnessed a few blocks away — we both just sat there for a minute. His years as a journalist gave Leon an ability to cut through the bullshit that few people possessed.

"It was definitely the Resistance that shot at you," he said.

"Yeah, that's what I think."

"Definitely. The Gestapo part of it still has me puzzled, though. Are you sure you aren't giving yourself away somehow? That's the only reason I can figure why they would keep letting you go."

I had been over it in my head countless times, and now I went over it again — but out loud for Leon's benefit. There were a small group of Resistance council leaders who knew our last two sabotage targets. I guess it was possible that one of them was working for the Gestapo. But the problem was, the only people who knew the escape plans for the two operations were Little Max and me.

"So let's say Little Max broke under the pressure," I said.

"Little Max?" Leon said. I explained about the two Max's at the telephone exchange building job.

"So let's say he was tortured and told the Gestapo," I said. "Or let's say he has been a traitor all along — although there's no fucking way that's true. But let's say it is. What's the point? They still let us blow up the targets. And they still keep letting me go even though I know that I'm not the traitor and they know that I'm not the traitor. And they still let me see Vogl, and they let Vogl see me. And besides, where's Max?"

"Little Max?" Leon said.

"Either Max. They're both missing." And then I explained about the pants with the hem that had given up on one leg. I was able to tell him the story without breaking down in tears, although it was close. And then we were just quiet again.

"I don't know," Leon said, finally. "I just don't know. It's like they're just playing with your head."

"Exactly," I said.

"And it's obviously working."

"I feel like crying. I feel like crying all the time — and I'm just so goddamn tired. But look — you have to listen."

I began to sketch out for Leon how my problems had now become his problems. To me, the smaller issue was the Resistance. Marcel knew about me and my involvement with moving the Jews, and if he decided to tell the council, they could potentially use Leon to get to me.

"But I really think that's a minor worry," I said, and he agreed.

The much bigger issue was the Gestapo. The problem was my Allain Killy identity. It was under that name that the flat was rented. And because of that, it was under that name and address that the Allain Killy ration cards had been obtained. The way you signed up for rationing was to go to the neighborhood municipal building, and fill out the paperwork, and show your identity card. Because everybody needed ration cards, that register in each neighborhood was the most complete and accurate listing of who lived where in Lyon. They could find the address of the flat in a half-day, after six or seven phone calls.

"So whenever they decide that they've had enough fun," I said, "the first place the Gestapo will go is our house. Manon will tell them that I have left her, and they'll search and see that my clothes closet is empty and there is no sign of me there anymore. Hopefully, they'll leave her alone. But then they'll make their six or seven phone calls—"

"And they'll be here by lunch," Leon said.

"Exactly. If you're lucky, you and your latest new family won't be here. Speaking of that," I said, and arched an eyebrow.

"I told you, just the couch."

"Her idea or yours?"

"Mine," he said. "Truly. And if you would stop worrying about my sex life for—"

"Worrying about your sex life used to be one of my greatest pleasures," I said. "Christ, where has that life gone? Are we ever going to get it back?"

We had some decisions to make. Really, Leon did. I told him that I would be willing to continue funding the identity cards with Marcel.

"You really trust him that much?" Leon said.

"It's a gut feeling — but yeah, I do trust him. At least I think I do. Whatever — I'm willing to keep taking that risk, until I can't. But what about you? You have to take the risk with Marcel, too — unless you want to arrange a hiding place where you would leave the photos and information for the next group and I could pick it up."

"It can't be here, though," he said.

"No, not here. Maybe if I gave you the address of my new flat—"

"No," Leon said. "I don't trust myself. I could get followed. Or if I got caught here, I could give up the address if they beat it out of me. I don't trust myself."

"I'd trust you with my life, but you might be right," I said. "But I don't have another hiding place handy. And you and Manon are the only two people in Lyon who I trust right now, and we're not going near her. Agreed?"

"Agreed," he said. "So if you're willing to risk it with Marcel, so am I."

"But what about the flat? The Gestapo is going to come at some point. We both know it."

"Not if they catch you first," he said, smiling.

"And on that cheery fucking note —"

"Look," Leon said. "This is a new risk, but it isn't a crazy risk. Yes, they'll come at some point. But if I keep this thing going, how many days a month will I be here? Five or six, tops. That leaves 25 days when they might come and find the place empty — in which case, they would probably go on their way and keep looking elsewhere. So, what, 5-to-1 odds? Shit, that's nothing. I'm 5-to-1 to have a heart attack while I'm sitting on the toilet these days."

We talked about a couple of other things, including the fact that I wasn't going to be able to keep restocking the cupboard. As for paying the rent, I was going to leave an envelope for Isabelle with two months' worth on the way out. In the kitchen, the dishes had been cleared and Myrna was playing Slap Jack with the kids, and they were howling in mock pain with each blow that was delivered. It almost seemed normal.

"Look, I have to run and beat the curfew," I said. "I don't know when I'm going to see you again."

And then we hugged, and we both cried. After I scooped up whatever clothes were in the closet, I think I cried half the way back to the new flat. I was walking as quickly as I could without seeming too conspicuous — although, honestly, people hurrying home to beat the curfew were a common sight and not conspicuous at all. Anyway, I made it by about 10 minutes. And then I slept for about 12 hours. It was just before I faded out that I remembered that I hadn't eaten anything all day except for the bit of stale baguette when I was hiding in the traboule.

30

I woke up with a hangover. It wasn't an alcohol hangover because I hadn't been drinking. It was either a slept-too-long hangover or a didn't-sleep-enough hangover, not that it mattered. I needed to get up and make some decisions. First, though, I needed to eat something.

It was technically illegal to barter your ration coupons for money or goods or anything, but everybody did it. Few were willing to trade away their staples, their meager allowances of meat or fat or bread, but most everything else was negotiable, especially two things: wine and cigarettes.

I didn't smoke, which gave me an enormous advantage. The ration was two packs of cigarettes every 10 days, but only for men. The ration for wine was one bottle every 10 days, for men and women. Because the cigarettes weren't nearly enough for those with the addiction — four smokes per day barely kept their hands busy for an hour, and that was if they didn't share with their wives — those people were an easy target. The typical arrangement was for a drunk to trade his cigarette coupon for a wine coupon. Nobody was happy with the situation, but it was how you got by.

I typically traded my cigarettes for wine, too, although I liked to think I wasn't a drunk. But this time, I needed food. I had the cigarette coupon and I had cash. The biggest black market was way up by the Hotel de Ville. It moved around a bit, away from the shadow of the enormous fountain featuring the enormous woman with the enormous breasts, and the Gestapo sometimes raided the area. But I didn't want to go up there.

There were smaller black markets in every neighborhood, near the municipal buildings where you signed up for the ration cards and picked them up every month. I had seen the Saint-Fons building the previous day on my walk, and when I got there, the furtive knots of desperate men, talking and then walking into an alley to make the coupon exchange, were plentiful. The Gestapo could have scooped up a handful at any time if they so desired. It was just one more indication that the farther away you got from the center of the city, the less likely you were to find trouble.

I joined the first group of men I encountered and said I needed food for a cigarette coupon, but nobody was interested. You had to be a special kind of addicted to the smokes to make that kind of deal, given that they said the ration cards would give you 1,300 calories a day, but most people thought it was more like 1,000, and everybody's clothes were hanging off them. But I found a guy and we struck a bargain which we consummated in the alley: my cigarette coupon in exchange for a cabbage, a few grams of meat — likely two pieces of bacon — a baguette, and a bit of coffee.

Back in the flat, I fried up half of the cabbage and one of the pieces of bacon. It was tastier than I had expected. That, along with half of the baguette and a cup of the ersatz coffee — barley and chicory and sawdust, for all I knew — were a feast, and I still had the other half for dinner. After cleaning up, I picked a bit of bacon out of my teeth and almost felt human. Then, with a second cup of the fake coffee, I went about the business of deciding my next move.

It came down to four questions. I laughed because the first three were the exact same questions from the last time, back in 1938:

1) Could I kill him?

2) Did I have the guts?

3) Could I possibly get away with it?

4) Would it be enough to convince the Resistance of my loyalty?

Back in 1938, the first three were the questions I asked myself repeatedly as I decided whether to try to kill Werner Vogl. Back then, the fourth question concerned my Uncle Otto, and whether I would be able to understand why Vogl had him killed. This time the fourth question was different, and it was more important. Because I needed positive answers to both No. 3 and No. 4 if I were to have any chance of resuming a normal life, not that anything was normal in Lyon in 1943. There was no way I could survive an existence where both Vogl and the Resistance were after me. Really, I couldn't survive either of them being after me for very long, not all alone. As long as I was in danger from either of them, I couldn't be with Manon or the baby. And that wasn't a life I wanted to live. That just wasn't an option.

So I kept up the mantra, trying to be as systematic as I could:

1) Could I kill him?

2) Did I have the guts?

3) Could I possibly get away with it?

4) Would it be enough to convince the Resistance of my loyalty?

Back in 1938, the first two questions were the hardest. I had never killed anyone, except for maybe an anonymous Italian in the war — and from such a distance that I never really knew either way. I was a spy, but really only a courier who took military information from skeptical German officers across the border and into Austria, hidden amid all of my traveling salesman's paperwork. I was frightened enough that I was ready to quit a couple of times, and I was more than concerned that Vogl was on to me, but it wasn't until I found out that he had arrested my uncle and had him killed that I thought about revenge.

It was so out of character that Leon laughed when I first told him. But Otto's death changed me in ways I never anticipated. And when he stopped laughing, Leon admitted that my plan for killing Vogl wasn't bad. And I would have killed him, too, had not the Abwehr interrupted at the last second and used me to frame Vogl in their own plot.

Since then, I had killed once in Zurich and three times in Lyon. I had convinced myself that each death was necessary in the end. I knew that Vogl's death was the most necessary of all. I knew I could do it. I knew I had the guts. Part of me knew that I really had no choice. And the more I considered it, the more I believed that the Resistance would see the killing for what it was, a sign of which side I was really on.

That left No. 3.

Could I possibly get away with it?

PART III

31

Our little Resistance cell had only seven people in it — and that was if you included Leon as one of the seven. One was Lucianne, whose father had operated a loom in the silk factory next to Manon's father. But he was dead, and her husband had been killed in the early days of the war in Belgium, and Lucianne was both committed to fighting the German occupiers and uniquely positioned to help — because her day job was working in the post office of Gestapo headquarters on Avenue Berthelot.

Early on, when the council was trying to decide which Resistance cells to include in their little fucking club, it was Lucianne whose work did more to convince them than anything — more than, you know, Manon's newspaper and me blowing up bridges and rail lines for them, me financing it myself. Assholes. Anyway, from her work in the post office, Lucianne was able to collect personal information on many of the Gestapo officers who were stationed in Lyon.

For most, she was able to learn their faces when they picked up their mail — and, later, to match those names against the photos of random Gestapo officers that were being taken from a flat across the street from the front gate on Avenue Berthelot. With the occasional extra bit of digging — and it really wasn't very hard, given that these were men away from home who were either desperate for or dreading contact with the people they left back in Germany — Lucianne was able to add some family details to the names and faces. And when the handbills starting turning up all over Lyon — with photos of otherwise anonymous Gestapo sergeants, revealing their names and their wives' names and their children's names — the Germans, in Max's best expression, "shit the fuck out." You had to be there. Even if they increased their roundups of suspected Resistance fighters, it was worth it to get so thoroughly under their skins. All we ever saw them do was strut. For that one, brief, glorious stretch, they were on their heels.

Anyway, the council talked about those handbills for weeks. That was about three months earlier, and Lucianne had been forced to lay low after that, so as not to attract any suspicion. But now I needed her, and I intercepted her as she walked home after work.

She was surprised and happy to see me. She greeted me with a hug and a kiss on both cheeks. I had been worried about approaching her, but that fear quickly ebbed. My concern was that she somehow had been told by a person in the Resistance that I wasn't to be trusted anymore. I knew it was a small concern — the cells were individual and isolated, for the most part, with only the leadership in joint contact — but it was still a possibility. Then her hug told me that I had nothing to worry about because Lucianne might have been a capable spy, but she seemed incapable of faking that kind of emotion.

We caught up as we walked, and then I said, "Look, I need your help with something." Her look suddenly became serious, almost fearful.

"I don't know," she said.

"Are they still all worked up about the handbills?"

"No," she said. "That's calmed down. But I haven't done anything since then, and I'm just worried. I feel like I just barely escaped — they questioned all the girls who work in the post office. It wasn't hard questioning — they did it altogether in a group — but they said things like, 'We need you all to be watching everything and everyone, including each other.' And they threatened us."

"Threatened how?"

"Just this," Lucianne said. "They said that if they found out that anyone in the post office had betrayed them, that they would arrest not just that girl, but the rest of us, too."

She was scared. I understood completely.

"Here's what I need — and it's nothing like the last time," I said. I was doing the best I could to undersell the danger, and it was the truth. Mostly.

"Do you know the name Werner Vogl?"

"I'm not sure," she said. "I don't think so."

"I just need you to find out everything you can find out about him, and to do it in the next two days."

She started babbling, flustered, about the timing. I stopped her, and put my hand on her arm, and said, "Please try to be calm. It's not like the last time. We're not going to put his picture on handbills on the street. We're not going to tell anybody about this. This is just the two of us, just you and me. But for a future operation, I need everything you can find."

"Future operation?" she said.

"Not your concern. Just get me what you can — and don't write anything down. Just do it from memory. You don't have to dig anywhere that you shouldn't be digging. Just whatever you can find."

"In the next two days?"

"Yes," I said.

Lucianne had calmed down some. She had access to his mail, to any wire he might receive, and to his pay information — that was how the Gestapo got paid, at the post office, and that was where they might be sending some of their money home.

"Just try to memorize anything you come across," I said. "And that's really it. Don't go out of your way — just whatever you happen to see. Remember the name — Werner Vogl."

"Do you know his rank?" she said.

"He was a captain a few years ago, but I don't know now."

Lucianne's fear seemed to have subsided. The simplicity of the task was apparent. There really was no risk, seeing as how it was her job to deal with all the information I was seeking. I told her I would meet her in two days, on the same walk home.

32

D espite my nonchalance, I wasn't sure if I was putting Lucianne in danger or not. Before I intercepted her on the walk home, I wanted to be sure that she wasn't being followed. It wasn't going to be that easy, given that Avenue Berthelot would be lousy with people headed home from work at the same time. But I was pretty sure she wasn't being tailed and then, when she stopped to buy a baguette on the way home, I was positive. It was the best and easiest way to stop a tail, stopping and shopping, and she was clean.

I met up with her on the next block. The sidewalk wasn't crowded at that point, but it wasn't empty, either. There were two men in business suits walking about 20 feet ahead of us, and two teenage girls maybe 50 feet behind us. It was perfect, really. We did the hug and the kissing of the cheeks as if we hadn't seen each other in a long time, just for show — but I really didn't think anybody was watching.

"So?" I said.

"Your Werner Vogl is interesting," she said. Her smile suggested he was dirty-interesting.

"Meaning?"

"He gets letters written in a feminine hand from two different places," she said. "Berlin and Frankfurt. The one from Frankfurt was vaguely scented."

Vogl was a stick-up-the-ass, no-nonsense Nazi, but he did have both a wife and a girlfriend back in 1938 — he wife in Berlin, the girlfriend in Frankfurt. It was the only sign that he was short of perfection, and the Abwehr used it as an element of the scheme to frame him as a traitor. The story was too involved to tell Lucianne, though. It would have taken 15 minutes. I stuck with the basics — the girlfriend was the scented letter from Frankfurt.

"There's another thing," Lucianne said. "He sends them both money every month."

"Who gets more?"

"Same amount to each," she said. "Shithead."

This was fascinating, but I couldn't imagine how it might be helpful. I didn't know what I was looking for, but that wasn't it.

"I was able to take a peek into his file — we share space with the records people," she said.

"One big happy Gestapo family."

"It was a quick look," Lucianne said. "I was able to make him a duplicate pay envelope, and three other duplicates for three other officers. We get them empty and fill them with their pay. But I told the file clerk that the totals seemed incorrect on all of them and I needed to see their pay grades in the files. She made some crack about how all we ever do is save other people's asses, and handed me the files, one by one. I could only take a quick scan."

"Anything interesting?"

"From what I could see, he was transferred from Cologne in 1938 and suffered a loss in rank," she said. "It didn't say why. He was transferred to Berlin, and he worked in administration for a while. Then I saw he was in Poland before he was here. But that was it. It was about a five-second glance."

"Is he a captain?"

"Yeah," she said. "Somewhere along the way, his rank was restored. But don't ask me where."

I had figured as much. I never really believed they were going to ship him to Dachau after the Abwehr fit the frame around him. The politics of the Gestapo vs. the Abwehr was such that I always thought he would be protected by his own people somehow. As for the Poland part, I already knew that. It was all helpful in completing the picture of Vogl that I already carried in my head, but that picture wasn't going to help me kill him.

"Anything else?" I said.

"He lives in the Hotel Terminus," she said. "But almost all the officers do. Nothing special there."

When she was done, I acted about a thousand times more enthusiastic about the information Lucianne had brought me than I felt. Her smile told me how proud she was to be a part of the Resistance, and of this "future operation." I thanked her profusely and told her to lay low again for a while.

"No risks," I said. "Be extra careful. The most important thing is for you to keep the job. I'm sure there will be another operation soon."

I really hoped that I hadn't endangered her, and that her bogus pay packet scheme wouldn't draw any attention or suspicions. Because the truth was, she didn't give me shit. The truth also was that I had no reason to believe she would be able to supply me with anything but shit when I asked for her help, and that I had put her at risk for no reason.

33

The clock at the top of the Perrache station's facade said it was 8:10 a.m. I think they kept it a minute or two fast. For nearly three weeks, Monday to Friday, I had walked through the train shed at pretty much the same time every morning, in the one open side and out the other. Sometimes I bought a newspaper as it could be part of the disguise when I was dressed as a businessman in a suit. That day, though, I didn't. I was in my priest outfit, and carrying a small satchel, and that would be sufficient.

It was my favorite disguise, mostly because nobody ever looked a priest in the eye. I take that back — little children sometimes did, pointing and occasionally laughing. "Look Mama, that man is wearing a dress." At which point she would drag the pointing child in another direction, and shush him, and maybe slap his hand or the side of his head. But she would never look at my face. Nobody ever did.

Once I was through the station and out the far side, the Hotel Terminus loomed on the left — solid, stone construction, substantial. The Terminus was the Gestapo dormitory, and all the officers lived there. They had their offices there at the start, too, before expanding to larger quarters on Avenue Berthelot. I wondered whose job it had been to clean the blood spatters off of the gold brocade. And did they feed the lopped-off fingers to one of the house cats or just set them out with the nightly garbage?

I had grown confident over the weeks, probably too confident. But the disguise really was perfect. With my hair dyed gray, and a big pair of glasses, and the black cassock, and the black hat with the wide brim — it was like a small version of a Mexican sombrero — I honestly didn't recognize myself. There was no way that Vogl would recognize me, not that I would afford him the chance. He tended to walk to work on nice days, and this was a bright and clear morning, but I still had a few minutes before he came out. I approached the bell captain, who was standing at a small podium just outside the front door.

"A question, Monsieur?" I said. And, like everyone else, the bell captain looked more through me than at me.

"Yes, Father," he said. "We have no rooms, if that is your question. We are booked full with—" Then he stopped and just pointed at the red Nazi flags that had sprouted on numerous poles surrounding the hotel's main entrance.

"Oh, no," I said. "I could never afford this, even if it were available. Can you point me toward the cathedral? My accommodations will be there."

He pointed north and said it was about a mile, and I did begin to walk that way. But after a block, I made a right turn and headed east. Then I doubled back and waited about a half-block from the corner. As if on cue, maybe five minutes later, I saw the man in the Gestapo captain's uniform striding purposefully across the intersection. I followed him, maybe 300 feet behind.

From the hotel to Avenue Berthelot wasn't much more than a half-mile. It was a 12-minute walk at an easy pace most days, but Vogl was moving a little quicker than normal. We were on

Cours de Verdun Recamier, headed in the direction of Pont Gallieni, one of the bridges over the Rhone. The bridge connected directly into Avenue Berthelot. The Gestapo headquarters was on the second block from the river. The complex, in the old army medical school, was on the right side of the street.

I obviously knew where Vogl was going, but I was trying to be as thorough as possible, even given the fact that I was scared shitless whenever I was on the street. The new flat had been a godsend — I actually felt safe there — but the streets remained a terror. I couldn't do it without the disguises, and Vogl wasn't even the main reason for that. The Resistance remained just as big a threat, and theirs were faces that I mostly did not know.

The hair dyes were a big part of it. Every night, in the bathroom sink of the flat, I changed the color — from my natural light brown either to black or gray. I had two pairs of eyeglasses containing plain glass, one with a heavy black frame, the other with a thinner gold frame. And I had a hat to go with every disguise — and two hats to go with the priest disguise: one the sun hat of a country priest and the other a more traditional biretta that you saw priests wear around the city. Since I had never been much of a hat wearer, except in truly shitty weather, the hats alone were plenty disguising. Among other reasons, they were all a half-size too big, at least. One of them — the businessman's Trilby, sat so low that it perched on my eyebrows.

I had four disguises all together. The least-disguising was the typical laborer's outfit, although the tan flat cap helped. I wore that one the least. The businessman's dark gray suit with the Trilby really was pretty effective, mostly because of the hat but partly because it was the most common look on the street in the morning near the hotel. Besides, I could use the newspaper as more camouflage, if necessary, because every suit was carrying either a briefcase or a newspaper or both. Still, I had never felt the need to hide behind the paper. I really was pretty careful.

The priest outfit with the bigger hat was my favorite although I tried not to overuse it. And then there was my street cleaner's get-up, which I bought off of a guy who was beyond down-and-out. I gave him enough money to eat for a month on the black market — or, in his case, enough to drink for maybe two weeks. In exchange, I received some stained coveralls, a beat-up hat, a small dustbin on wheels, a broom, and a shovel. When I asked the guy how he was going to live without the tools for his job, he said, "I'll be honest, I just stole them from someone else."

Rotating through the disguises, wearing a different one in the evening than I wore in the morning, I gave myself three weeks to study Vogl's habits. I decided to skip the weekends and concentrate on Monday to Friday. I had started on a Tuesday and ended three Mondays later. The final Monday was the morning I was wearing the priest outfit with the big-brimmed hat, and it was fairly typical.

On nice days, Vogl would leave the hotel at right about 8:15 and walk the same way. If it was raining, or just crappy, he would sometimes get a ride. But when he walked, the route was identical — down Cours de Verdun Recamier, across Pont Gallieni, pause for a few seconds to wait for the cop in the middle of the intersection to stop traffic so he could cross Avenue Leclerc, and then down Avenue Berthelot. He was at the front gate of Gestapo headquarters at 8:27 most days, and likely in his office by 8:30.

More days than not, he would leave work at 4:30. But the problem for me was that while Vogl did have habits, they weren't entirely consistent. The weather affected his decision to walk or be driven, but that was a relatively predictable variable. His work, though, could bring him into the office later than 8:30, and it sometimes kept him there well into the night. He stayed as late as 8 p.m. on two of the 15 nights. One night, I wasn't sure when he left because I gave up to get home to my flat and beat the curfew. And then there was the day he never showed up at Avenue Berthelot at all.

In the three weeks of watching, I was able to identify only one constant. It was on Fridays, and it was in the morning. It didn't matter if it was raining, or sunny, or overcast and blustery, because the same thing happened in all three weather conditions.

At 8:15 on every Friday morning, Werner Vogl came out of the front entrance of the Hotel Terminus and walked to Avenue Berthelot. But on those three days, and only those three days, he had a companion. And while I could never get close enough to be 100 percent sure, I was reasonably certain that Vogl's companion was Klaus Barbie's dog, Hildy, tethered on a thick leather leash.

34

Because it had been more than three weeks, I needed to go back to Marcel's shop and check on Leon's side business. I told Leon I would keep the money flowing, and it was a promise I intended to keep, even if I was so scared during the walk that I nearly pissed the cassock.

I did my espionage due diligence, walking past the shop on the opposite side of the street, checking in another shop window for a potential tail, walking another block just to make sure, and then right, left, right, and left before finally coming back upon Marcel's door. I didn't feel a tail, and I was dressed as a priest besides, so fuck it — which wasn't much of an attitude for a man of the cloth but, well, fuck it.

"Ah, Father, what brings you to my humble shop today?" It was clear that Marcel didn't recognize me, so I decided to play along.

"A gift for a friend," I said.

"And what are your friend's interests?"

"It's hard to pick just one, because Leon is a man of many and varied interests," I said. At that point, Marcel stopped looking through me and started looking at me. It still took him a second, and then he just said, "Well, fuck me."

"Fine way to speak to a priest." He stepped from behind the counter and walked around me in a circle.

"Jesus Christ, I can't believe it."

"Again with the language."

"Goddaaam," he said, and then Marcel whistled as a form of punctuation.

I wanted to hug him but held off. It was the best I had felt in a while, just knowing how effective the disguise was. I was pretty sure, but you can never completely trust yourself. This was confirmation. I felt relaxed, and suddenly really needed the bathroom. Marcel pointed, and I didn't hesitate.

When I returned, he got right down to business.

"You just missed him," Marcel said.

"Who?"

"Leon," he said. "About an hour ago."

"Did he say anything?"

"I gave him his latest packet. It was literally an hour ago. He said they're on the afternoon train to Marseille — 4 o'clock, I think. And he gave me the next batch — a woman and a 10-year-old boy."

I opened my little travel bag and took out the payment for those next two identity cards. I now had an opportunity to see Leon, but did I dare chance a meeting at the flat where they were hiding? I wasn't sure, and I had time to consider. As I counted out the money on the glass counter, Marcel stopped me, mid-count.

"You know, they're after you," he said. And while I knew exactly what he was talking about, I played dumb.

"They?"

"The council," he said.

"You know about the council?"

"Of course I know," Marcel said. "There aren't many people in regular contact with people from *Combat*, from *Liberation*, from your place, whatever it's called. But I happen to be one of those people. In fact, I might be the only person. It's a unique benefit of my chosen profession."

"So—"

"So you know they're after you, right?"

"Yeah," I said. "The bullets they shot at me were a fair bit of confirmation."

Marcel scooped up the money off the counter and put it in his special drawer. He fiddled with something else in the drawer that I couldn't see. It crossed my mind that it was a gun. But whatever it was, he left it where it was and silently closed the drawer.

"You know, I'm supposed to turn you in," he said.

"Will you?"

"I'm supposed to, Father. I was specifically asked to keep an eye out for you. They asked if you had been in the shop recently, and I told them no. So that was a lie. But I'm not sure I want to get into the business of routinely lying to those people. I mean, I have a skill that they need, but I'm not sure lying to the Resistance is a smart strategy in the long term — mostly because I'm not sure there tends to be much of a long term for such people."

Marcel said that the Resistance had actually told him about a designated letter box in a certain building where he was to leave a message if I had been in the shop.

"I was to attempt to make a future appointment with you — for delivery of a new identity card, presumably," he said. "But in any case, I was to leave them a message, if not with a future time than just with these words: 'The two-faced coin is in stock.'"

"That's pretty hokey."

"That's what I thought, but it's their game, so it's their rules."

"So what are you going to do?" I said. "I mean, will you?"

Marcel stopped as if he were thinking — not deciding, not exactly, but just trying to come up with the justification for whatever decision he had already made. It was as if he had gone over it in his head enough times but hadn't quite found the words. When he began speaking, it was as if he was groping for those words.

"If you were coming in for papers for yourself, I might," he said. "If it was just you, trying to get new papers so you could disappear, I might turn you in. Sorry, but I might."

"But that isn't wh—"

"I know, I know — and that has made it harder for me, more complicated. But that's what I keep coming back to. You're not doing this for yourself. These papers, none of them have been for you. None of them have been for your family. The risks that you have running here — the risks that you are still running, even though people are taking rifle shots at you—"

"You knew they were rifle shots?" I said. With that, we both smiled.

"I told you that I talked to everybody," he said. "But that's it. The risks you have run, that you still run, they are not the risks a traitor would run. That's what I keep coming back to."

"So maybe you could tell them that."

"I can't."

"Why not?"

Look, this is a tough time," Marcel said "Shit, I don't have to tell you that, but it is. It's just tough. There is mistrust on about eight levels — different factions, different ideologies. I hope I'm not insulting you, but those fucking Communists give me a headache — but I cannot get involved in that. You run risks, I run risks. I think we both do it for the right reasons. But I can't get myself in the middle of your shit."

But we both knew he was getting himself in the middle by

keeping my secret. And when I began to speak, it was with a true feeling of gratitude.

"Look, I appreciate—"

"Enough talk," he said. And then he walked down to the end of the counter and pulled out a wax paper envelope full of loose stamps. "I don't care what you're dressed like, you still need to buy something, just in case. And I went out and got some cheaper merchandise, just for you."

He looked down at the pile.

"The cheapest one," I said. "I'm on a priest's salary now."

"There was a time I would never have permitted shit like this in my shop," Marcel said, plucking one out and putting it into an envelope of its own. He really did appear to be disgusted.

35

I thought about going to visit Leon at the flat, confident as I was about the priest disguise, but then I thought better of it. There was no reason to be cocky. I could just arrange to run into him at the train station. It was a little counterintuitive, but a public meeting was safer than a private meeting, given everything.

I would need some kind of train ticket, just in case, so I bought one to the second stop on the same train as Leon and his guests, the night train to Marseilles. In all likelihood, I would just throw it away after we were done talking.

So I bought my ticket and parked myself on a bench. I had managed to purchase a priest's breviary from a second-hand bookstore, just to complete the disguise, and pulled it out and began reading. Well, not actually reading — the book was written in Latin — but pretending to read. I had to remind myself to turn the page every few minutes.

From what I gathered, priests were supposed to read from it every day. And given that I now paid close attention to priests who were in public, but from a distance, it seemed that they all had their noses in the book whenever they had a spare minute.

On one of my businessman-in-a-suit days, I sat down next to a priest on the very same bench and interrupted his reading, asking how long it took him every day.

"Most days, two-and-a-half hours," he said. "Some days, three."

"Wow. It's like another job."

"But remember," he said. "I don't have a wife to listen to at night."

Neither did I. And while I had managed to avoid the almost daily temptation of going to see her, I wasn't sure how much longer I could hold out. The truth was, I was really thinking about going that night. As I was thinking, Leon arrived on the platform with a woman who was hand-in-hand with a little girl, maybe 5 years old.

Leon walked within two feet of me and did not react. When I stood from the bench and said, "Please, sit," he thanked me but still did not react — not immediately. It was only after they were on the bench that he saw through the disguise. So I sat again, and the four of us looked like what we were, people chatting on a bench in the train station. And within a minute or two, after introductions were made and explanations offered — no, I wasn't really a priest and, yes, Marcel told me where to find you — the conversation was just between him and me.

"What's with the dress?" Leon said. And with that, I explained what I had been doing for the previous three weeks.

"Because?" he said.

"You know why," I said.

"Fuck no, not again?"

"Yes again," I said. "Remember the last time I told you."

We had been in a bar in Vienna. He was waiting for a source who might or might not have had a tip on a story, and he laughed when I told him I wanted to kill Vogl — like, literally laughed. But as I explained the reasoning, and detailed as much of the plan as I had sketched out in my head, he warmed at least a little to the idea. But the irony of the scheme — that is, that I was the careful one and Leon was the daredevil, and I wanted to take the risk and he thought it was crazy — would always stick with both of us.

Five years later, though, a lot was different — about each of us personally, and about our lives, and about the hell we lived in — and it was as if we no longer were permitted the luxury of personal irony.

Instead, as Leon listened to my idea that killing Vogl would not only get him out of the way but also convince the Resistance of my loyalty, he just said, "Have you figured out how you're going to do it?"

The truth was, I had not. I had promised myself to do three full weeks of reconnaissance and to keep an open mind, and I had just finished, and I had not yet synthesized everything we knew. I was about to give him the summary of my surveillance of Vogl when we were interrupted by two black uniforms and a single question: "Papers, please."

This was, I immediately realized, the flaw in my priestly disguise. I was dressed as a civilian in the picture on my identity card and was not identified as a priest. My only hope was that these two Gestapo mugs had never seen a priest's identity card, either.

I dropped the breviary as I stood up to reach into my pocket. The uniform said, "No, not you, Father."

I sat back down. The identity cards for Leon, and woman and the child were passed to the uniform. He moved a step away to get a better look beneath an overhead light. As he did it, he blocked the view of the other goon. And in that instant, I looked at Leon and he mouthed one word: "Louis."

He once told me he was Louis in every one of his fake identities, and that is what I would have guessed. Now I had some confirmation, and a bit of room to maneuver.

"And how do you know these people, Father?" the uniform said, turning his attention back to us.

"I have seen my friend Louis here in church, but not as often as perhaps I should see him, isn't that right?"

Leon looked at me and then dropped his eyes.

"You're right, Father," he said.

"And them?" the uniform said. He looked down and eyed up their identity cards for a second time, cards bearing I-had-no-idea-what names.

"I have also seen them in my parish," I said. "But I am relatively new there and don't know all the names. But the child is strikingly beautiful, don't you think? Dressed on Sunday, you can imagine she looks like an angel. So when I saw them walk by, I invited them to sit with Louis and I. A small parish meeting from Saint Marie's. We are all on the same train, too. Imagine the coincidence."

"Tickets?"

Fortunately, they were for three different stations along the line — mine first (I was using it as a bookmark in the breviary), then Leon's (to a station where he would transfer on the line back to Paris), then our Jewish friends (who were going further south). Satisfied, or at least satisfied enough, the uniform handed everything back, and he and his partner walked over to scare the shit out of the people sitting on the next bench.

At which point, we all exhaled. The three adults instinctively congratulated the little girl on her performance, although the truth was, we all likely felt a bit emboldened by surviving the cursory check of our papers — or at least I did. But as the train approached the station, I was worried that I would have to use my ticket and ride the one stop for no reason, lest the two Gestapo goons see me leave and suspect something. But then, with a single warning blow of the train's whistle, the two of them hurriedly hopped across the track to the opposite platform. The train would block their view, and I would be able to get out after all.

The Jews said a round of thank-yous as we stood up. Leon and I hugged, but there were no tears this time.

"I want to help if I can," he said.

"I don't know—"

"Listen. If you come up with a plan that needs an extra hand, I can help. I want to help. It's the least I can do."

"I think you have enough risk in your life."

"Maybe," Leon said. "But if this works, you eliminate Vogl and you eliminate the suspicion of the Resistance at the same time. How can I pass up the chance to see you kill two birds with one stone? Isn't that what the English say?"

I had no idea, but I liked it.

36

I was tired when I arrived at the door of the silk factory. It had been a long day on my feet including the last two miles from the station, the last bit straight uphill to Croix-Rousse. But I was convinced I was invincible in the priest's get-up. Leon's initial inability to recognize who I was had been the last bit of encouragement that I needed. My life was only going to get more dangerous, at least in the short-term. Here and now, dressed like Father Alex, was my last, best chance to see Manon before I went about the business of trying to kill Werner Vogl.

I knocked our special knock, and I could hear her running to answer. She opened the door slowly and dragged me inside and hugged me immediately. I mean, there was no way I was going to fool her. We hugged, and then we kissed, and then she began to work a couple of the buttons on the cassock.

"Here," I said, let me pull it over my head."

"No, just a couple of buttons," she said.

"Really? Some fantasy of yours?"

"Maybe."

"Isn't that against the rules?"

"Who are you going to tell? When was the last time your ass was in a church?"

I had a lot to tell her when we were finished and re-buttoned. She was almost done printing the latest edition of *La Dure Vérité*, and wanted to get finished before she went home, so we sat in the little store room in the back and talked over the Roneo, which hummed when it wasn't clattering and clattered when it wasn't humming. There was a loose bit of something in the machine's innards, but I had no idea how to fix it.

I realized I hadn't told her that the Resistance had tried to kill me. I knew she would be wild when she heard, and she was. She exploded with a string of invective that was brutal, even for her, including the memorable "if it was that motherfucking ass-grabber, I swear..."

But she calmed down almost as quickly as she erupted. She asked for more details, took it all in, nodded. "Yeah, it was definitely those assholes," she said. "I mean, what else do we have to do—"

"I know." I was trying to be rational even though I shared every bit of her sentiment. "I know. But why doesn't matter, and the fact that they're wrong doesn't matter. They're trying to kill me, and I have to stop them. And because of that, I have to get out of here. Like, in five minutes."

Manon grabbed my hand, but she knew I was right. A priest had showed up at the silk factory after work hours. If anyone saw it, and thought about it for more than a second, a phone call could lead to another phone call, and to trouble. So I didn't have much time to tell her about my plan to kill Vogl.

Again, she put aside her emotions and listened intently. She was a professional spy, after all — or at least she had been at the start of the war, before she grew sick of the incompetence of her bosses in Zurich. She understood why I'd spent three weeks attempting to discern a pattern in Vogl's activities. She immediately dismissed the idea of doing anything to him after his work day was over.

"It's too erratic," she said. "You could never plan something and be confident it would take place. And you can't leave your ass hanging out too long here. It has to be quick."

"So you agree?"

"I don't know the plan yet because you don't know the plan yet," she said. "But the concept, yes. I agree. It scares the hell out of me but, yes, I agree. Because the way you're living now is no way to live."

"We could just try to make a run for it," I said. "Back to Switzerland. Or to Spain."

"I don't run," she said. "You know that."

"I know, but with the baby—"

"We don't run," she said. "Besides, you've already been chased from Austria to Czechoslovakia to Switzerland to France — and Vogl is still there, still after you. Enough. You'd have to get to America to get away from him — and what are the odds? No. And I don't run."

We talked some more about what I had seen. She agreed with what had become my preliminary thought, that the time when he was walking the dog on Fridays likely made the most sense because it was the most predictable.

"Night is best," she said. "It's better than in the morning. Nothing there? Nothing at night? No pattern at all? I know he leaves work at erratic hours, but is there no cigarette on the front steps of the hotel before bed? Nothing like that?"

"Sometimes he goes out to eat," I said. "At least I think it's out to eat. A driver takes him somewhere at dinnertime and brings him back about two hours later. But I had no way to follow him in a car. And it was only twice in three weeks."

"No, that won't do — not enough information and too random," she said.

"Look, I really should go," I said, the plan unresolved. I looked over at the Roneo, which was finished. I leaned in for a whiff of the paper and Manon said, "Like every schoolboy."

We were avoiding the obvious, and neither of us spoke the words as we hugged in parting. The truth was, this might be the last time we ever saw each other. If the plan went well, and I killed Vogl, and I was able to escape detection, and I was able to convince the Resistance of my loyalty, Manon and I could be together again. But that was a lot of ifs, a string of contingencies. If even one of them failed to fall into place, we could be done. I could be dead, or on the run. And Manon had made it more than clear that she would not run.

Into the silence that we shared, I broke the hug, gestured at the Roneo and said, "Let me take a bundle."

"Well..."

"The usual?" This was a reference to the used bookstore without a name on Rue Romarin. The word "BOOKS" was stenciled on the plate-glass window in the front, and that was it. The woman behind the counter was named Marie, no last name. That was all I knew — other than that there was a big delivery slot in the back of the store, big enough to accommodate an oversized book. We would drop a tied bundle of the flyers through the slot, and she would handle distribution in the neighborhood. Marie took care of about 25 percent of our print run that way.

I tied a bundle with some twine. Manon said, "You're going as the priest?"

"You might be right," I said. "It's bad enough to have been seen on the way in as a priest. On the way out would be worse. There are some coveralls here, right?"

And so, dressed as a silk weaver who had just worked some

overtime at the factory, I left with a small cardboard satchel filled with *La Dure Vérité*. I felt almost naked without the priest disguise, but at least it gave me something to worry about — better than thinking about how I had tried to memorize every line and imperfection on Manon's face in the last few minutes I was with her.

37

It wasn't curfew yet, but I still decided to travel to Rue Romarin through the traboules. Because while there was no reason for the Gestapo to stop a man carrying a small suitcase as he walked the streets of Lyon before curfew, there was no prohibition against them doing it, either. There really were no rules anymore, other than that they made the rules up as they went along, and there was nothing anybody could do about it.

So when I walked in the first door at Cour de Vaces, I just looked like somebody who lived in one of the apartments. And then I began my journey of repetition: down the 10-or-so steps, into the little courtyard at the base of the surrounding buildings, across the courtyard to one of the exits, down another couple of steps and through a dark passageway, out the door that led to the next narrow street, then across that street and into another nondescript door, then down another 10 or so steps.

Over and over, that was the journey down from the hills of Croix-Rousse into the center of the city. For some reason, I allowed myself to take in a few of the details along the way — I guess because I didn't feel as if I was being chased. And if I sensed any danger at all, there were a dozen places to hide the little suitcase in one of the traboules — behind one of the big earthenware planters in the one, planters that held palm trees, of all things; in the wooden box containing gardening tools in another; or maybe behind on a hook behind the wool tapestry that hung on one wall. I looked behind it to see if there was a hook and there was.

There were traboules in old Lyon that were more beautiful than the ones in Croix-Rousse, mostly because old Lyon was once a truly wealthy district while Croix-Rousse was always working class. But the traboules in Croix-Rousse were still beautiful in their own ways, mostly because of those little touches inserted by the current residents, like the palm trees and the tapestry. But what really hit you was what they represented: the whiff of danger. If Max had been right, they were not about the architecture or about keeping the silk dry as it was transported down to the river. If he was right, the traboules were about the nefarious, and had been for centuries.

I actually took my time — there was still plenty of time before the curfew. I could drop the flyers at the bookstore and easily be home to the flat. So it was actually a nice stroll, down and down, into the Cour de Vaces with the beautiful stone staircase, out on Montee Sainte-Sebastien, through the narrow street passage and in on Rue Imbert Colomes, then out on Rue Des Tables Claudiennes, then in and out again on Rue Burdeau, down and down, then out on a street I still didn't know and back in to the next house across the way, then out on Rue des Capucins, then across the street and in one more traboule, where the exit was on Rue Romarin. I opened the final door and the street was dark and deserted. There were so few people out at night anymore, even early in the evening. No one had any money to spend, and none of the restaurants had any food worth spending it on — and forget the bars. It was almost impossible to get drunk in Lyon anymore unless you made the wine yourself in the bathtub.

The bookstore was one block down on the right. The lights were off in the front but, after I walked between buildings and to the back door, the light was on in the back of the shop. Then I saw Marie on the back steps, feeding two alley cats. She heard me and looked up, and I could tell that she recognized me before I could speak.

"You keep feeding them and they'll never go away," I said.

"Kind of like you people," she said.

I opened the suitcase and took out the bundle of flyers, leaving the cassock and the bashed-in hat. She held it in her hand as we talked. I asked about the danger of distributing the flyers and she shrugged.

"One of the benefits of being an old woman is that no one looks at you for very long," she said. Old women and priests, then. Who knew?

"I can easily take about 20 or 30 sheets a day," she said. "They fit nicely in the inside pocket of my coat. And even if there were a few lumps, well, who thinks twice about the lumps in an old lady's coat? I have some regulars who I know want them, and the rest, I just stick them in mail slots, or maybe leave one in the slats of a park bench. This stack will be gone in a week, no problem."

"Do you think it makes a difference?" I said. It was the question I always asked myself, because other than Manon and one or two others, I never knew anybody who actually read what Manon put out. It was almost impossible for either of us to gauge the reaction. Was it meaningful, or were we shouting into the wind? We just didn't know.

"Here's the way I look at it," Marie said. "I have people who ask me for it and ask when the next one is coming. So those people are reading. I know that for sure. If they pass it along to somebody else — and I tell them all to do that — then between those second readers and the people who just find it in their mail slot one day, I think yes. I think it makes a difference. We all need something to hold on to. We all need some sign of hope. That's what these are," she said, holding up the bundle. "They're hope."

"I can't tell you how much it means to hear that," I said. My voice cracked at the end, as I thought about how happy Manon would be to know what Marie had said, and wondered whether I would ever be able to tell her.

"Put it this way," Marie said. "I wouldn't take the risk if I didn't believe it was helping. I mean, I might be old but I don't have a death wish."

I left her with the bundle, and the cats, and with a kiss on each cheek. I still had time to get home to the flat, but I had to get to the journey. Curfew wasn't for an hour and there were about two miles to walk. It wouldn't be a problem, but I needed to get started, especially if I wanted to give myself time for the odd detour, just to be sure I wasn't being followed.

I walked back through the alley and turned right onto Rue Romarin. I hadn't walked for two minutes when the black Citroen pulled over next to me, tires squealing, and the two uniforms invited me to sit between them in the big back seat. The black trench coat in the passenger seat welcomed me with, "Nice to see you tonight, Herr Kovacs."

38

We drove for about five minutes, south from the center of the city into the old part of Lyon. Other than the initial greeting from the trench coat, using my real name, no one said anything. Traffic was less than half of what it used to be even during the day, given the scarcity of petrol, and it was almost non-existent at that time of night, so close to the curfew. The only other car that we passed was another black Citroen, and each honked to the other as a greeting.

The car stopped in front of an old bouchon. I didn't know exactly where we were, but I did see a church steeple looming behind the restaurant. I think it was Saint George's. The light from the restaurant shone through the big front window and splashed onto the sidewalk. There appeared to be a half-dozen tables occupied, most in twos and threes, all in black uniforms. In a world of rationing, the Gestapo were the only ones who routinely ate well.

The two uniforms and the trench coat escorted me inside. I was taken to the only table that was occupied by a single individual. It was Werner Vogl.

"Alex, Alex, please join me," he said, half-standing then returning to his seat. The napkin was tucked into his shirt beneath his chin, like a bib.

"Thank you, gentlemen, that'll be all," he said to the three henchmen who had transported me. They were gone and I was sitting there, right near the front window, and Vogl was waving for the waitress to bring me a plate.

"No thank you," I said. It was half-hearted, though, and Vogl told the waitress, "No, leave it. He might change his mind."

It was an old place, as the bouchons tended to be. Rustic did not begin to describe the main dining room. The ceiling was held up by rough, exposed wooden beams — but they had been haphazardly reinforced in places. The table were all the same, about 30 inches square, but the chairs were mismatched, some cane back, some solid, all worn. The floor was made of wood planks, the wood in a bit better shape than the ceiling beams. For decoration, a wagon wheel hung on one wall.

In the center of the room, there was an iron spiral staircase — down to the kitchen, up to a loft. When I asked to use the bathroom, Vogl said "certainly" and pointed me up the steps, where the loft contained the toilet, about 10 more tables, and an impressive wave of hot air that had risen from the kitchen and though the main dining room.

There also was a private dining room on the main floor as well as a small bar. When I came back from the bathroom, every time I saw someone look in as they scurried past on the way home before the curfew, I so wished we were in that back room rather than in the front window. There was an ancient grandfather sitting on an elevated stool behind the bar, and he was sleepily taking in everything, too, especially me. The waitresses were a mother and daughter who sounded as if they were quietly bickering about the daughter's latest boyfriend. It was a running argument playing out over time, a few words here, a few there, in between restaurant conversation about water pitchers and bread baskets. But they, too, were looking me up and down. Vogl noticed, too.

"You do seem to be attracting some attention," he said. "I guess they don't get many civilians in here anymore."

The food was plain, delicious and massive. Just the bread basket, with real butter, would normally have fed me for two days. The salad Lyonnaise made me want to cry — lettuce, other greens, onions, two quarters of a tomato, croutons, a beautiful poached egg on top and enough bits of bacon mixed throughout — real bacon, meat not just fat, some in every bite.

"Are you sure?" Vogl said, as they took the half-eaten salad and brought the next course. I just shook my head reflexively.

The quenelle that came next was perfect. Big and fat, cooked in its own dish, swimming in a sea of cheesy fish sauce just made for the bread to wipe clean. Served along with a big plate of grilled vegetables and a mound of rice, crowned by a dollop of tomato sauce.

Then came the dessert. It was crème brûlée, the sugar burned on top. Sugar! You needed cream and eggs to make the creme which meant it was impossible to make in Lyon in 1943, but the burned sugar on top — well, let's just say that you couldn't duplicate it with saccharine.

He offered again. I declined again. But when the waitress brought the coffee, I couldn't resist. I had not had real coffee in months, maybe a year. I missed it more than the wine sometimes. One cup, I figured. It was only a small sin.

"Finally," Vogl said. "Here, here, have some cream with it."

Coffee with cream. Okay, two small sins. I think I might have moaned after I took the first sip. But Vogl snapped me out of my brief ecstasy.

"So, Alex, it has been too long," he said. He wasn't smiling anymore. "In case you were wondering, the Gestapo never believed the result of that little trial we had. They protected me from any real punishment. And after a few months, all was forgotten."

I wanted to tell him that I already knew that, but thought better of it. There was no advantage to be gained, and only the possibility of raising his antennae. I took another sip of the coffee instead. I don't know what it said about me, but I was staring at my potential executioner across the table and still determined to finish the coffee before it turned cold.

"So I had a choice," Vogl said. He began talking about Fritz Ritter, the Abwehr general who was really the traitor to Germany, the old friend of my uncle who used me as bait in an elaborate frame-up of Vogl. I had not seen Ritter since 1940 and wondered if he were alive or dead. When Vogl kept referring to him in the present tense, I was slightly cheered.

"I could either go after him and get my revenge that way, or I could go after you," Vogl said. But Ritter was too complicated a maneuver because he was traveling constantly with the Abwehr and because the Abwehr rivalry against the Gestapo would always add a layer of protection.

"You, on the other hand, were unprotected," he said. With that, he inhaled an impolitely big spoonful of crème brûlée and then wiped the corners of his mouth with the bib.

"Unprotected," he said again.

Other than to ask for the bathroom, I'm not sure I had said much of anything since sitting down. If he was waiting for some kind of reply, I had none. He was right — I was unprotected. I thought he didn't know the half of it, that I was in both the Gestapo's sights and the Resistance's sights. But I shouldn't have been so naïve.

"You're probably wondering by now," he said. "You're wondering why we keep arresting you and keep letting you go. You're wondering why I just looked at you out of the window that day. It's really simple. I'm going to get my revenge by letting your own people kill you."

I had considered this, in my most despairing moments, but had rejected the notion because the Gestapo were never about art. They were about brutality, and they were about delivering the brutality themselves.

But this was Vogl, who used to attempt to offer academic comparisons to me between the Roman Empire and the Third Reich. He was, I had to admit, a different kind of Nazi. Thinking about it, and about him, it all began to make sense.

"You know, we're sitting so near the window for a reason," he said, pointing out toward the street. "The Resistance keeps track of us everywhere. I know that, Barbie knows that — he eats in public restaurants, too, just to taunt them. They walk by the windows and take attendance whenever I am here. It is the same faces every time. They think they are so clever, but I don't care. And now they have seen you. And at least a few of them have seen you drinking coffee. And one or two more will see you leaving by yourself in about five minutes.

"Twice now, you have been released from Avenue Berthelot while your sabotage partners have been beaten or even killed."

I tried to resist asking, but I couldn't.

"Max?" I said.

"The young kid? The one who called you Pops? You will be happy to know that he fought to the end. Vive la France. Whatever." Vogl sipped his coffee. "Very foul mouth, that one."

Goddamn. I suddenly felt sick to my stomach. Only some of it was my feeling for Max, though.

"I'm going to let your own people do it," Vogl said. "They've seen you released twice now. They will see you leave this bouchon in a minute after sharing a meal with me. It won't be long now."

He paused. "I know they already tried once," he said. The

look of surprise on my face must have been evident, because he immediately followed up with, "You're surprised that I know? That actually hurts me, that you would think I didn't."

Vogl stood and indicated that I should do the same. He yanked the bib out of his neck and shucked on his uniform jacket. He walked me to the door, out on the sidewalk, out in the open, and he hugged me.

"Laying it on a little thick, aren't you?" I said.

"Nonsense. It's the perfect picture. You know someone is watching, and when he tells the story, it's all that he'll talk about."

By then, I had extricated myself from the embrace. But one final time, Vogl leaned in and whispered in my ear, "This is much more fun than just having one of my men cut your throat. That is simple violence. This, this is art."

39

Big streets, no hurrying, no hiding — that was the walk back to my flat. No evasive tactics, no circling back, no looking behind me — that was how little I cared. Because I really didn't care, not about the curfew, not about anything. And as it happened, I never saw another black Citroen the whole way.

If I had really been able to think about it, been able to strip away the maelstrom of emotions in which I was struggling, what Vogl had told me was actually good news on a couple of levels. First off, I wasn't crazy because they *had* been toying with me. I didn't have all the details down, but my sense had been correct all along. They were fucking with me, and now I knew the reason why. At least my instincts and my sanity were intact. It was a small comfort, but what the hell.

But there was something else, too. I had lived for nearly a month believing that two different entities were trying to kill me, the Gestapo and the Resistance. What Vogl had just told me cut the number of potential assassins in half. Because the truth was, at least in the short term, the Gestapo wasn't after me. They didn't want to arrest me, or torture me, or kill me. Instead, they wanted to leave me naked on the streets, prey for the Resistance. And while the Resistance was more dangerous than the Gestapo in some ways, because of their greater numbers and their relative anonymity, it wasn't as if the Gestapo was a bunch of weekend amateurs when it came to violence. So eliminating them from the let's-kill-Alex playing field was significant.

But it also was temporary. It really was a short-term reprieve. I mean, it had to be. Because Werner Vogl had a boss, a fellow named Klaus Barbie. And while Vogl had apparently been able to convince Barbie to play it his way, it was hard to believe that the man with the fourth-floor torture chamber above his office would sit still for too long while Vogl's twisted scenario played itself out. I didn't know how long I had before the Gestapo came after me, but it wasn't forever. My guess was two weeks, but it was only a guess.

But it was a guess that I didn't make for a while. It took hours before all of this dawned on me — it was the next morning, in fact. On the walk back to my flat from the bouchon, I didn't have that capability yet. I was in a complete fog. I nearly got run over by an empty bus that must have been heading back to the garage. It was noisy, and belching smoke from that wood-burning contraption on the front, and it was the only vehicle on the streets, and I still walked right in front of it. The driver slammed on the breaks and swerved, just barely missing me. He actually got out of the bus and began cursing me. I just mumbled a few sorry's and continued on south toward the flat.

I didn't have the ability to string together a series of coherent thoughts, to game out different scenarios. I really felt like I was drowning, and there was this noise in my ears that distracted me whenever I tried to concentrate on any single aspect of my predicament, a noise that wouldn't go away.

Because while I wasn't naïve — I had seen evil before, experienced it, lived within the midst of it — I had never seen someone get as much pure joy out of evil as Vogl had at our dinner. It was stunning, and I was stunned, and I couldn't shake it. Killing your enemy in a war made sense to me. Even if your motives were evil, as the Nazis' were, there was a certain basic understanding there. Even the terror of torture, well, I got it. You were after information, you had no morals, you cut off a finger — and if they didn't tell you what you needed to know, you cut off another finger. It was inhuman, but there was at least a line of thinking, that you would do whatever it took to get the information you needed. It was all an exercise of power.

But what was Vogl doing? He wasn't seeking information. He wasn't simply seeking revenge, either. No, what he was doing was torturing me for fun. He was taking pleasure out of my terrible predicament — a predicament that he'd created. It was as if I were a wounded rabbit stuck in a cage with a badger — and not only had Vogl wounded me and put me in the cage, now he wanted to watch. The whole purpose, it seemed, was to give him that chance to watch. It was as if he got off on it.

And that, I had never experienced. The inhumanity of it made it hard for me to catch my breath. It was only the next morning when it dawned on me that Vogl might be a sick and evil bastard, but it was because he was a sick and evil bastard that I was still alive and still had a chance.

40

Sleep was what I needed. I was days behind, not merely hours. If I could just pass out, I believed things would be better when I woke up. It was the only concrete thought I could hold in my head as I entered the building and walked up the stairs to my flat. But when I reached for my key, I quickly realized I wouldn't be needing it. The door of the flat was wide open.

I walked in and dropped the suitcase at my feet. I couldn't believe I still had it and the things inside — the cassock and hat, the eyeglasses and the breviary. Neither the Gestapo goons who picked me up on Rue Romain nor Vogl said a word about it or looked inside. Vogl might have taken a peek when I used the bathroom, but that would have been the only time. And he never said anything about it. If he had looked, I'm sure a wisecrack about the cassock would have been in order.

The place was ransacked, entirely torn apart. Drawers pulled open and emptied on the floor, the mattress on the bed and the cushions on the couch turned over — and, in the case of the cushions, the zippers unzipped and the stuffing pawed over and half removed. The saving grace was that the place was barely furnished, and that I really didn't own shit. There was only so much mess the Gestapo could make.

One thing they did see, though, was the disguises. Not the priest outfit but the rest of them — not that they would think much of either the business suit or the standard work clothes. Even so, the pockets had all been pulled inside-out. The street sweeper's coveralls and implements appeared to have gotten a closer inspection, but they were all still there. The dustbin on wheels was turned on its side, but nothing was broken.

Still, they had seen the hair dye in the bathroom, and the second pair of eyeglasses, and the collection of hats. My first thought was that I was going to need a new disguise if I was to kill Vogl. But that thought was rapidly overtaken by the need for sleep. The lock was broken, but I was able to close the door. I think I was asleep 30 seconds later.

The knocking that woke me came about 12 hours later, at 10 a.m. — knocking, followed by yelling, followed by the hem of a dirty housecoat in my face, just at the side of the bed. Needless to say, it was my landlady. Just then, I realized that I didn't know her name, not that it was going to be necessary. She hadn't taken a breath since she had begun yelling, and even though she lowered the volume once I opened my eyes, the words continued to tumble forth and the message was clear.

Or, as she said, summing up, "You've got two hours to get your fucking ass out of here."

I sat up and thought about pulling up the sheet to cover me, but then I realized that while I had managed to wriggle out of the coveralls, I still had on underpants. I wasn't completely naked. So, fuck modesty.

"And you're not getting your deposit back, either," she said. "Did you see how they broke that goddamn lock? No, no deposit back. No fucking way."

I wasn't arguing. I wasn't saying anything. But with all of her yelling, the cobwebs had cleared in what might have been a personal record for me. As soon as I saw the break-in the previous night, I knew I was going to have to find a new place, so all of her yelling didn't matter to me. But I needed as much information from her as I could get before leaving.

"So the Gestapo, what time—" I said, but she stopped me.

"Gestapo? What the hell are you talking about?"

I waved my arm at the drawers dumped on the floor and the couch cushions in disarray.

"It wasn't the Gestapo," she said.

"Local cops? Lyon police?"

"Those jackasses? No."

"Then who?"

"Figure it out yourself, Dr. Freud," she said. There was a slight pause and a look on her face that mocked me, and then she continued.

"It was the Resistance," she said.

"How can you be sure?"

"What are you, retarded? They weren't German — they were French. They weren't wearing uniforms — they looked just like you or me. Do the math, Euclid." And then she paused again and spat one more word: "Imbecile."

I got it. I really wasn't stupid. It's just that my first thought was that it had been the Gestapo, and that was the thought my subconscious had carried through my 12 hours of sleep. The new information was jarring. And if the net-net analysis of my night with Vogl was that his little game was not all bad for me, the fact that the Resistance found me was the opposite. It was entirely, 100 percent bad.

"They banged on my door when they were leaving," she said.

"Did they know my name?"

"They called you something different — Allain something,"

she said. "So I could tell them the truth, that I didn't know you by that name."

"Did you tell them the name on the lease?"

"Of course," she said. "What do I owe you? But I did lie a little. I said I hadn't seen you in days, almost a week. I also said I thought you were using the place for a love nest, which is what I thought at the beginning, the day you signed the papers. But you haven't had any pussy up here, I know that. So I lied about that."

"Anything else."

"They had a picture of you," she said. "I stared at it a long time and said it could be you, but I wasn't sure. I went back and forth, and I think I ended up saying I didn't think it was you. So, another lie." She paused, then spat out again: "You're fucking welcome."

I really had nothing to say to her. I certainly wasn't going to thank her. She filled the silence with a final, "Two hours," and then she turned and left, slamming the door behind her. Because the lock was broken, it bounced halfway open and I watched her stomp down the stairs.

I had nowhere to go other than the second flat, the one where Leon hid the Jews — because there was no way I could go back to Manon. I knew Leon had just gotten on the train the night before, so it would be empty for at least a couple of weeks. Seeing as how I didn't have a couple of weeks, but realistically only a couple of days, that would be plenty.

And so, dressed as the street sweeper, I put all of my shit into the dustbin — the knapsack, the suitcase, the disguises, and the rest — and wheeled my way west and then north. I beat the landlady's deadline by 20 minutes.

41

I walked into the building and walked up the stairs to the flat. Just as I got near the top, Isabelle met me on the way down. I could see behind her that she had left a pie on my doormat. I felt like kissing her, and so I did.

She blushed.

"Oh, Herr Killy, it is only a pie," she said. Because she was deaf, she yelled the words at me. I yelled back in return. It was like trying to communicate while standing in the terraces in Pfarrwiese in the seconds after SK Rapid scored the go-ahead goal. My God, when was the last time I was there, 1938 — back in Vienna, before the Anschluss, before everything?

"It feels like salvation," I said. The words seemed to have less meaning, less of the tenderness that I felt, when bellowed. "What flavor?"

"Apple," she said.

I kissed her again.

"I guess they liked the sandwiches," she said. I had not noticed that she was carrying an empty, clean plate until she lifted it up to show me. "Not a crumb left behind."

"They?" I said. My surprise might have raised my reply even

a few decibels beyond bellowing. She just looked at me and smiled and shook her head, like a schoolteacher who couldn't believe my inability to comprehend the day's lesson.

"Yes, they," she said, just as loudly. "I might be deaf, but I'm not an idiot."

And then I just hugged her and didn't let go. The plate was wedged between us, jabbing my ribs, but I didn't care. When we moved apart, I needed to find out more. Part of me worried that someone would hear — we were shouting at each other, after all — but these old places were stone fortresses. There was no way anyone on the street could hear what we were saying. At the very worst, someone right outside the heavy wooden front door might be able to discern that voices were being raised, but that was it.

"How long have you known?" I said.

"Almost since the first time I saw that other handsome friend of yours," she said. "Like I said, I'm not an idiot. Children can't sit still — and even if I can't hear them, I can feel the vibrations. Toilets flush, baths run. This old house speaks, even to those with bad ears."

"How long have you been feeding them?" I said. I pointed to the plate.

"This is the first time," she said. "I have a friend who helps me trade the coupons I don't need, the wine coupons, but Andre can't always come over."

"Andre?" I said, smiling a naughty smile.

"Again, Herr Killy, I might be deaf, but I am still a woman."

My wish was to adopt Isabelle as my grandmother. If only I had an identity that wasn't compromised.

"I also have a friend on a farm who can bring me a jar of the fruits she has put up for the winter."

"Another friend?" Again, with the naughty inflection.

"Enough with your dirty thoughts," Isabelle said. This truly sounded hilarious when yelled as loud as a roaring airplane engine. "My friend on the farm is like a sister to me. She might get here once a month or so. That is when you get your pie."

"Did you see them, the people in the apartment?"

"Just for a second," she said. "The adults didn't see, but one of the children opened the door a crack while I was sweeping the stairs. I saw her for a second, and then she saw me and closed the door as quickly as she had opened it. Pretty little thing. Jewish, yes?"

I nodded.

"It is what I assumed when I saw your handsome friend. Jewish, yes?"

I nodded again. I was wondering why Leon had not mentioned that Isabelle knew they were there, and that she was feeding them. It seemed that he didn't know that she knew, and as for the plate of sandwiches that Isabelle had left on the door-mat, he must have just figured that it was sandwiches this month instead of a pie.

"Are you okay with this continuing?" I said.

"I don't know what 'this' is. And I don't want to know. I can guess, and that is enough, and yes, it may continue for as long as you want."

I just looked at her. Bravery and patriotism come in the oddest packages sometimes. Isabelle Vaillancourt, 80 if she was a day, deaf as a post, defying the law and the Gestapo to save a bunch of Jews she had never met and never would meet.

"I can guess what you're thinking," she said. "Your face betrays everything — I would like to gamble with you sometime. But it isn't what you're thinking. I'm really not in any danger."

"Of course you are," I said.

"I am 82 years old. I am deaf. Everybody who knows me knows that I am deaf. If the Gestapo comes to my door, they will find me, 82 years old and deaf. You could be running an illegal munitions factory out of that apartment and I would still be 82 years old and deaf. They wouldn't arrest me. They would just assume that I knew nothing."

She stopped, frowned, then smiled. It was as wistful a moment as you could imagine, except for, you know, the screaming of the words.

"Being old, being deaf, people assume I'm dead," Isabelle said. "In most instances, that is a sad thing. But in the case of the Gestapo, it is an enormous benefit."

She invited me into her apartment for a cup of ersatz coffee. We each used it to wash down a slice of the apple pie, which was anything but ersatz. We didn't say much, sitting side by side, me on the end of the sofa, she on a comfortable side chair, her feet propped on an ottoman. Soon she closed her eyes and fell asleep. I covered her with the blanket that was folded on the arm of the sofa and let myself out as quietly as I could. I was in the bed and almost asleep myself when I thought, why had I been so quiet? She's deaf.

Still, I felt protected somehow. One more good sleep, I figured. One more good sleep, and then I needed to make a plan. The cautious part of my personality was battling with the scared-shitless part of my reality, and scared-shitless was winning because, well... because it needed to win. Caution was not a luxury that I was permitted any longer. This was Tuesday. I needed to kill Werner Vogl on Friday.

42

For the 16 hours after I left Isabelle's flat, I was either asleep, taking a bath, or eating apple pie. At dawn on Wednesday, I smoothed the creases out of my business suit the best I could, hanging it on the curtain rod in the bathroom as the tub steamed below it. Then I put it on, along with the Trilby that sat low enough to touch my eyebrows, and walked to the police precinct where Raymond worked. On the black lamp post directly across from the front door of the station house, I made a mark with a piece of yellow chalk. It had been weeks since Raymond and I had agreed on the signaling system, and this was the first time I had used it. I could only hope that he was still checking every day.

The reason I needed to talk to Raymond was simple. Every incarnation of a plan to kill Vogl that I had been able to concoct had one fact at its foundation: the need for a weapon. Specifically, a gun. I didn't know of any way to obtain one, other than from Raymond — and if I couldn't get one from him, I needed to find out immediately so that I could make another arrangement. Seeing as how any such arrangement likely would involve somehow stealing a gun from someone, the potential complications were obvious.

I wouldn't know if Raymond had seen the signal until 9 p.m. up at the Roman ruins. In the meantime, I figured more sleep was as valuable as anything else I could be doing. But before that, I decided to take one more peek at Vogl's morning routine.

I walked through the train station as I had the previous times I had been wearing the suit. I bought a newspaper and parked myself on a bench just outside the station, a couple of hundred yards away from the Hotel Terminus' flag-festooned entrance, so many red Nazi flags now framing the front door that it looked like the stage at a Nuremberg rally. We used to watch them on the newsreels in Vienna and marvel at the pageantry. Leon would see the lights and the flags and the rest of it and then watch Hitler climb the podium and say, "I bet he wears fucking stage makeup." I didn't doubt it.

From where I was, peering over the top of my open newspaper, I could see the front door with no problem. And if I wasn't close enough to pick out the face of a stranger, I would have known Vogl from twice the distance. I looked at my watch, and it was 8:05. I was 10 minutes early.

I watched for the next half-hour and Vogl never appeared.

With each minute, my blood pressure rose. I could hear my pulse in my ears. My plan was to kill the man in two days and I did not need a sudden change in his routine. It hadn't been perfect, though. That's what I kept telling myself. Other than Fridays with Hildy, there had been variations. There was no need to panic. This didn't mean anything unless, of course, it did.

At 8:40, I abandoned the watch and returned to the flat. Despite my nerves, I slept easily again, and finished the pie, and then began going over the details of the plan, as rudimentary as they were.

Finally, after dark, I began walking to the amphitheater. I hated the idea of taking the funicular up the hill to the Roman ruins because of the confined space. But the last time, I had walked up the hill and been seen by the Resistance and shot at — at least, I assumed that's when they saw me. Seeing as how there was no way to know, I didn't want to chance it again, so I would chance the confined space of the funicular. If the driver was in the Resistance, of course, I was screwed. But there was no way for me to avoid risk at this point, only to minimize it.

I got off the funicular and walked across the street and then up the smooth stone path to the amphitheater. Then it was up the steps, right up the middle aisle, until I got past the last row and to the top, where the paths and alleys that often led nowhere began. It seemed an especially dark night, and I had no idea where Raymond might be, until I heard a whispered "over here." Raymond was hidden in one of the alleys that went nowhere, over to my right.

"I almost pissed myself when I saw your mark," he said. "How are you?"

I told him. I told him everything. He pushed his hat up onto the back of his head and leaned against the stone wall and let out a long, low whistle. "Holy shit," he said, as if mumbling to himself, as if I wasn't intended to hear. "Holy fucking shit."

Then it hit him. "Wait, how's Manon?"

I told him that I had left her, for her safety, and he nodded in agreement. Then I laid out my plan, and I asked him what he thought.

"I don't fucking know," he said. "You act like I'm the chief of the department, for Christ's sake. I'm just a cop, just a fucking flatfoot. I swear to God, I directed traffic for four hours today. I'm not some tactician."

"I know, but you're not just some fucking flatfoot, and you know it. Tell me what you think."

"I guess it makes sense," was the best he could come up with. And that was after a full minute of silent consideration.

Then I asked him for the gun.

"Wait, a handgun?" he said, as if the possibility just dawned on him. "I thought you were going to shoot him with a rifle, from some distance. I thought you were good at rifles from the war."

"I was good at rifles from the war," I said. "But the war was a long fucking time ago. So I have no idea. And besides, I don't have time to set up a place to hide and shoot from. I need to do it now. I need a handgun."

"Well, I can't give you my service revolver," Raymond said.

"But how about your throwaway?" I said.

"You know about that?"

"Everybody knows," I said. A throwaway was the small pistol most police carried in case they needed to make the evidence align with the circumstances. If there were somebody who needed killing, for all the right reasons but without the legal niceties, a cop would kill him with his throwaway and then throw it away. Or, if there was confusion during a confrontation, and someone got shot who turned out to be unarmed, voila — with the throwaway, he was suddenly an armed man and the shooting was justified.

Raymond reached down to an ankle holster and removed a tiny revolver. He wiped it down with his shirt tail and then handed it to me. It really was small.

"You take this from a girl?" I said. "A baby girl?"

"What do they say about beggars and choosers? You have to remember, the Nazis got almost all the guns when they came in — only the people who had unregistered guns to start with could hide theirs."

"I'm surprised they let the cops have guns at all," I said.

"Most don't. But here's the Germans' secret: if we had them

already, we could keep the guns, but not the bullets. I have three bullets for my official gun. I think yours has four. I guess I should have told you that."

A pea-shooter with four bullets. I was so fucked.

"Seriously, how close would I have to be to kill somebody with this?"

"Three feet," Raymond said. "Five tops."

"Man—"

"Give me a day, and maybe I can get you a rifle," he said. "Let me see what we have in the evidence locker. I might be able to turn up something."

"I don't have that kind of time," I said. "And besides, I really might not be able to shoot for shit anymore. The last time I did it, I was 18."

"Are you sure?" he said, and then he pointed to the pistol. "Three feet. Three fucking feet."

"Five tops," I said.

43

My original thought was to kill Vogl while disguised as the priest, out of some perverted sense of good karma. Plus, I really believed that the black sombrero was the best disguise I had. But when I thought about it, I realized the disguise wasn't as important before the shooting as it was after. The odds were, I would go unrecognized by anyone on the street either way, seeing as how I didn't plan to be on the street for more than five minutes or so before I pulled the trigger.

Afterward, though, was going to be the issue. And while I could wear the business suit under the cassock, which I would ditch at the first opportunity, I couldn't really carry the Trilby while wearing the cassock — and, to me, the Trilby was the only real camouflage that the business suit provided. But if I went as the street cleaner, I could wear regular clothes underneath the orange coveralls and carry the flat cap in the dustbin. But then I thought some more and figured, why couldn't I carry the priest's get-up in the dustbin and change to that? The only issue would be having to grab the knapsack holding the priest outfit from the dustbin when I ran. It would have to be in the knapsack because fleeing with the dustbin just wasn't feasible. So that's what I did.

On Friday morning at 7:30 a.m., I had positioned myself on Quai Claude Bernard. It was the street right along the river but on the other side of the Rhone from the Hotel Terminus. When the time came, I could lean against a tree while pretending to take a break and watch the length of the Pont Gallieni, the bridge that Vogl would be walking across. But that would not be for more than a half hour, so I spent that time cleaning the street — sweeping and shoveling dirt, picking up stray newspapers that had been caught in the wind, and cigarette butts — although there weren't many of them, as people now routinely walked the streets with eyes down, searching for a few millimeters of unsmoked tobacco that someone had discarded. But whatever I found, I slowly went about the business of picking it up and disposing of it in my dustbin, right on top of my knapsack.

I made achingly slow progress up the street. If anyone gave me a second look, I didn't see it. Hell, if anybody gave me a first look, I didn't see it. Orange coveralls, dustbin, push broom, shovel — I was just a part of the urban landscape, no more interesting than a parked car. At about 8:10, I wheeled my contraption up onto the sidewalk and then onto the grassy stretch that separated the street from the river bank. There were some trees planted in the grass, not big plane trees but not spindly little shrubs, either. I leaned against one and attempted to light one of the cigarette butts I had recovered from the gutter. It was 98 percent filter and two percent tobacco, but it didn't matter. It was just part of the act.

On the three Fridays I had watched him, Vogl and Hildy left the hotel five minutes earlier than on his other normal days. That was to give Hildy time to sniff around and take a dump and still get Vogl to the office by 8:30. The other times, they had managed to take care of that before reaching the bridge. As it turned out, Vogl was not surprisingly more German than French in this regard — he curbed the dog rather than allowing it to take a crap in the middle of the sidewalk, as every self-respecting Frenchman seemed to do. Before the war, walking the streets of Lyon, or any French city, was like walking through a dogshit minefield.

The men just stop and piss along any wall they want to, and the dogs shit in the middle of the sidewalk — what a country. Of course, all of that was before the war. The men still pissed anywhere they wanted, but there really weren't any dogs in the city anymore, mostly because there was no way to feed them. By 1942, most family pets had been sold to heartless entrepreneurs who undoubtedly sold the meat back to the authorities as beef.

That was how my mind wandered until it got to about 8:20, which was when I saw Vogl and Hildy turn the corner and begin walking across the bridge. My heart raced, but I knew what I needed to do, and I began to do it. It was a pretty half-assed plan, but it was all I had.

And so, I walked along the quai and crossed the intersection, looking to my right and seeing the progress Vogl and Hildy were making on the bridge. I still had about 90 seconds to get into position. When the traffic cop waved me across, I hustled along with my dustbin. The cop yelled, "Slow down, old man. I'll hold it for you," and so I did slow down, a little.

I got to my spot on the sidewalk, just a few feet from where Vogl would cross to get to Avenue Berthelot. The street was wider than usual there, and a small traffic island that allowed right turns off the bridge made it just a speck more complicated than a typical intersection. I had never seen anyone not have to wait at least a few seconds before they crossed Avenue Leclerc, and a few seconds were all I needed.

I took a deep breath and fondled the baby revolver in the pocket of the coveralls. I looked back to the left and saw Vogl moving toward me. Ten seconds... five seconds...

They arrived at the curb, and Vogl and the dog did have to stop. I was close to them, maybe not three feet away but less than five. Vogl did not even look in my direction, fixated on the traffic cop, waiting for the signal to cross. But Hildy did see me. I don't know if she recognized me or if she just hated everyone, but she jumped at me and strained at the leash.

I panicked and shot her. And then it was all like it was in slow motion, except it must have taken about two seconds. The shot fired, and the dog fell. Because Vogl had been leaning away from us to brace himself against the straining leash, the sudden slack in the leather made him stumble a half-step backward. He looked down at the dog, lying on the sidewalk. The blood was already visible. And then, as it all registered, Vogl looked up at me. He looked beyond the orange coveralls and the beat-up hat I was wearing. He looked at my face. I don't know if I saw a sign of recognition or not. I don't know if it was a look of disgust, or half of a smile, or something in between. Later that night, when I closed my eyes and relived the moment, the face he made looked a little bit different every time.

Then I shot him. I got him up high, I was sure of that. But whether it was in the mouth or the neck, I just didn't know. I saw Vogl drop the leash and reach both hands up to the area of the wound. I had two more bullets, and I intended to use at least one more, but when I fired again, the gun jammed. At that point, I panicked and ran. My original intent was to drop the gun in place and walk away calmly. Instead, I chucked the revolver into the Rhone and sprinted away, barely remembering to grab the knapsack.

After the first shot, there had been no reaction that I could detect. Maybe everyone figured it was just an engine backfiring

— I mean, it wasn't as if I had fired a canon. But after the second shot, and after I began running, I did hear some yelling and the insistent whistling of what I assumed was the traffic cop. But I didn't look back.

I ran to the next block and made a left into Rue de la Méditerranée. A half-block down on the right, there was an alley that, at its end, connected to another alley off of the Rue Leclerc. I had scouted it out the day before, and deep into the alley, there was a small staircase leading to a basement door into one of the buildings. The staircase was hidden from the street. I had practiced slipping out of the orange coveralls, buttoning the priest's collar, and pulling on the cassock over my head, and I had gotten it done in about a minute, including changing to the black shoes and putting on the black mini-sombrero. It took me a little longer in the alley though, partly because I was shaking so badly and partly because I was performing my gymnastics on a nasty subterranean staircase.

But I got it done, and smoothed things as best as I could. I dropped the knapsack into one of the dozen garbage cans in the alley and the coveralls and shoes and hat into another and hoped they would go undiscovered. Then I walked out of the other end of the alley and onto Avenue Leclerc. I was wearing the big black hat, and I had put on the fake black eyeglasses, and I was carrying the breviary, and I walked right past Vogl's body, just on the other side of the street. That was always the plan, to walk right back into the scene, even to stop and gawk along with everyone else.

No one was near the bodies of the dog and Vogl other than the traffic cop, who looked helpless. It was as if people saw the black uniform and were actively keeping their distance. Most did not stare for more than a few seconds, and neither did I. I managed to cross the street and then cross again, and I was walking back across the same bridge that Vogl had just crossed when I looked back and saw a line of black uniforms running from Avenue Berthelot toward the body, which lay not two blocks from his office in Gestapo headquarters.

44

No one followed me, not past the Hotel Terminus, or through the train station, or all the way back to the flat. I had stopped shaking, but I was wired the whole way, my mind racing as I concentrated on keeping a leisurely pace, even stopping in a park for a few minutes to pretend to read from the breviary. When I finally walked into the flat, Leon was there.

"Why aren't you in Paris?" I said.

"It's good to fucking see you, too."

"But I told you—"

"I just want to help."

"Too late," I said. "It's done."

I told him everything as I changed back into normal clothes. I told him about killing the dog, and firing the shot at Vogl, and then the gun misfiring.

"You sure you killed him?"

"Pretty sure," I said. "I mean, I got him either here—" I pointed to my neck "—or here," and then I pointed to my mouth.

"Here would have been better," Leon said, and he pointed between his eyes.

"I know, I know. I would have with the second shot. But I was just so fucking scared."

"It wasn't meant as a criticism, I promise you that," Leon said. "I'm scared just thinking about it, and I wasn't even there."

We talked for a while, and then just kind of lay around. Leon had not been back to Paris in the four days since he had left Lyon. Instead, he decided to see the mother and daughter all the way to Toulouse, and then just retraced his steps.

"I wanted to see the other end," he said. "And I have to tell you, it is really inspiring. In Paris, there are so many people who don't give a shit, who just go along with the Nazis. They don't support them actively but they don't fight them either. They just go along. But to go to Toulouse and to see their end of the network — people risking everything for a couple of Jews they'll never see again — it really gave me some hope."

"You should look in a mirror sometime, buddy," I said.

"I could say the same thing about you," Leon said.

"Yeah, we're a couple of terrific fucking guys," I said, and then we just fell into silence. I think we both dozed off — I knew, with the adrenaline having ebbed, I felt exhausted again. I must have slept pretty hard because I didn't hear Leon when he left to go to the station to buy an afternoon newspaper.

It was only when he came back that I heard the door, and saw his face, and then heard him say, "They're saying Vogl's alive."

"But..." It was all I could come up with. Leon handed me the paper. There was a small article on the bottom right-hand corner of the front page, only three paragraphs, with the head-line, "Cowardly Attack Fails."

Witnesses are being sought to the shooting Friday morning of a

Gestapo captain and a dog as they were walking to work from the Hotel Terminus.

Captain Werner Vogl was seriously wounded but is expected to survive the attack, which took place at approximately 8:20 a.m. at the foot of Pont Gallieni, near Avenue Leclerc. A Lyon policeman said that a street sweeper was standing near the officer just before the incident, but that he did not see the shooting take place as he was directing traffic in the intersection. A wheeled dustbin, broom and shovel were found at the scene.

Anyone who witnessed the attack, or who has any information that may assist with the apprehension of the assailant, is instructed to report immediately to Gestapo headquarters on Avenue Berthelot.

I read it three times. The only reply I had was to keep repeating the words "expected to survive."

"That might be bullshit," Leon said.

"Might be."

"They might not want to admit you succeeded. It would be bad publicity."

"Maybe," I said.

"But even if he's alive, that doesn't mean he can communicate," Leon said. "You got him in a bad spot. He might be alive but in a coma."

"Yeah, maybe," I said. And then Leon asked the only question that mattered, the question that now crowded every other thought out of my head.

"Do you think he can identify you?"

"Maybe," I said. "Possibly. Probably. I just don't know. But as I'm fucking saying these words, you know what? It doesn't matter. If he thinks it's me — like, even if he thinks there's a 10 percent chance that it's me — he'll tell them and they'll come after me. Fuck, what was I thinking?"

"Look, it's done," Leon said. "For what it's worth, I believe that it was worth doing. And Manon told you she thought it was worth doing. And you thought it was worth doing. You can't second-guess it now. And if he dies without being able to say a word, you're in a much better position than you were 12 hours ago — much better."

"I guess," I said.

"I'm sure," Leon said. And it was an argument he repeated over and over, all through the night, all through a bottle of cognac that he had somehow scrounged from the Resistance group in Toulouse. I was just starting to believe it too, until Leon came back from a walk to the station for the morning newspapers. Because along with the newspapers, Leon brought along a flyer that he had ripped from a telephone pole just outside the station. It said, "WANTED FOR THE SHOOTING OF A GESTAPO OFFICER" in big black letters. And beneath those letters was an excellent likeness of me, likely drawn from the photo of one of my identity cards, or from Klaus Barbie's fucking memory, followed by this paragraph:

Alex Kovacs, a.k.a. Allain Killy, is wanted in the shooting of Gestapo Captain Werner Vogl. A reward is offered for information leading to his capture and arrest. All those with relevant information are ordered to report promptly to Gestapo headquarters on Avenue Berthelot.

"Well, I guess he's talking," I said, more to myself than to Leon. I had never received a bad diagnosis from a doctor, but I imagined that this was what it felt like. A little stunned, a little helpless — that was what I was feeling. At the same time, I knew I had to fight through it if I was going to survive. I had to think. I had to focus. And then it hit me. It apparently hit Leon at exactly the same time because we both said it simultaneously. We said one word:

"Manon."

PART IV

45

R aymond's house was a 10-minute walk from the flat. As I left Leon behind to pack up whatever he thought we might be able to carry, I knew I couldn't go right to his house — it wouldn't be fair to him or Marie or the kids, besides the fact that it wouldn't be possible to explain to the little ones why Uncle Alex was dressed up like a priest. I could just hear Lucy screaming as she ran to her bedroom, "Nooooooo. He's supposed to be a horse, not a priest."

It was beyond dangerous for me to even approach him, but I didn't see an alternative. I tried to guess what his walking route to the police station would be and I sat myself down on a bench in a little pocket park on Rue Garibaldi, me and my breviary and my toxic troubles. If I missed him, I would try him at the police station, which was exponentially more dangerous — assuming, of course, that the Lyon police would lift a finger to help the Gestapo. The truth was, they likely would do nothing. Then again, if I dropped myself into their laps, they might turn me over to Avenue Berthelot. It was a risk, but I just couldn't go near the house.

From the bench, I could see one of the wanted posters with

my picture on it, slapped on a telephone pole about 100 yards away. I looked at it, and then I pulled down the black mini-sombrero just a little tighter on my forehead. As it turned out, Raymond walked right past the telephone pole with my poster on it. It took him a full 10 seconds to recognize me when I began calling his name from the bench, calling it first in a stage whisper and then in a half-shout. No one was nearby, so it didn't really matter how loud I was.

"My God," he said.

"Yeah," I said.

"This is—"

"It's completely fucked up," I said. "But we don't have time to talk about that. I need a favor. I'm desperate." Raymond looked at me expectantly, and then he just lowered his eyes and nodded his head.

"Manon," he said.

"You need to go to our house and see if she's there," I said. "If she is, you need to make sure she knows, and you need to tell her to go into hiding. You don't have to hide her yourself — the Resistance will help her — but she needs to go right now. You can do that, right? You can tell her."

He thought for a second. I never had a doubt that he would do it — his relationship with Manon went back to their child-hoods — but he gave himself a little time to think.

"Okay," he said. He was about to play out the worst-case scenario for him. "If the Gestapo is there when I get there, I just tell them the truth — that she's my cousin and that I was worried about her when I heard the news. They'll buy that. I'll motherfuck you and say I never trusted you, and they'll believe it. All right. Let me go."

"Tonight at the amphitheater, 8 o'clock."

"Okay, okay," he said. "Let me go."

Our house was 15 minutes in the wrong direction, and he

began walking quickly that way, half-trotting. Even at that pace, Raymond would be late for work.

Meanwhile, I headed in the other direction, back to the flat. I didn't know where Leon and I were going to go, but we had to go somewhere. The more I thought about it, I couldn't believe the Gestapo hadn't come for me there overnight. It wouldn't take that long to find out which of the municipal districts was supplying Allain Killy with his ration coupons. Even though I had not picked up the last two sets of coupons, my name was still likely on some list, along with the address of the flat. Six phone calls, maybe seven.

When I turned the last corner, I saw the black Citroen parked in front of the apartment. It was the first one I had seen all morning. Nobody was inside the car. The front door of the apartment building was open with a Gestapo uniform standing half inside and half outside. I dared not get too close, even though the uniform's attention was focused inside, not outside. I was able to maneuver myself into the alley next to the building, though. And because the door was open, and because Isabelle was as deaf as she was, I could hear everything. The Gestapo voice's French was excellent.

"What is the name again?" she said.

"Killy. Allain Killy."

"No, that's not it."

"What's not it?"

"That's not the name," she said. Isabelle was playing the part of the addled old woman, and deaf besides. God bless her.

"What is the name?"

"I don't know. I mean, I forget things. But it was Marcel-something. I'm sure of that. Marcel."

If I had been able to see him, I was sure that the Gestapo agent questioning Isabelle was turning colors at that point. But he kept at it.

"But he's not here now?"

"No," she said. "Not for weeks. He disappeared, I don't know, maybe three weeks ago. It was rent day, and he was gone. I had already threatened to throw him out—"

"Why?"

"Women," she said. "I told him at the beginning: no women. This is not that kind of building. But there were women. I know there were."

"How do you know?" he said. "You can't hear anything, old lady."

"I might be deaf, but I'm not a fucking idiot, sonny," she said.

"Sonny?"

"Yes, sonny. What don't you understand?"

The Gestapo man was now officially irritated. He yelled at Isabelle to move, and she didn't. So he said, "You two — search her flat first, then we go upstairs." Isabelle cried out, and then I heard some broken glass. It all had been so loud, I only hoped that Leon had heard it, too. And when I made my way deeper into the alley and then around to the back of the building, I saw that he had. The window to my flat was open, and Leon's knapsack had already been tossed out onto the ground, and now Leon was worming his way out of the window. It was going to be a tight squeeze.

"Careful, slim," I said. He looked down. Leon was scared of pretty much nothing except for heights. I had seen him start fights and finish fights — big fights and one-on-one, bare-knuckled or armed with a broken bottle, drunk bar nonsense or street Nazis attacking a helpless Jew in Vienna — and never once saw him hesitate to get involved. He was as physically courageous as anyone I had ever met. But he wouldn't climb a ladder, not for all the money in your pocket.

"Thank God," he said, looking down. "You'd better break my fucking fall."

"Just hang on to the window sill and then let go." Which he did. I half-caught him, and we both ended up in a heap on the ground, unhurt. We hustled down the alley and hid between buildings farther down the block.

"First things first," I said. "What would be less conspicuous — you and a priest walking together or you and a normally dressed worker?"

"The priest is a better disguise, but I think a worker. But you need a hat."

He reached into the knapsack and pulled out a flat cap. "Yours? I grabbed everything I could find."

"Yeah, let's do it," I said. I slipped off the cassock and the collar, and just wore the work clothes that were underneath, and the glasses, and the cap.

Meanwhile, Leon hoisted the knapsack and groaned. I shrugged, and he replied, "It's heavy as shit. I grabbed every can of food that was left in the cupboard."

As we exited the farthest end of the alley, now a block over from the flat, he said, "So where are we going?" It was a pretty good question.

46

I couldn't be out on the streets for very long in the middle of the day. That much, I knew. Being with another person would provide me with some natural cover, seeing as how the Gestapo was looking for a lone fugitive who, if they were listening at all to Vogl, they knew was on the outs with the Resistance. But even with Leon, and the cap, and the eyeglasses, it was an enormous risk to be walking around the city. I needed a place to hide out and, the more I thought about it, Saint-Fons still made the most sense. All we needed to do was pick a different building with a different FOR RENT sign. It wasn't difficult to find one.

"I'm going to hide in the alley," I said. "Furnished, second floor, in the back. Here's some rent money. Don't haggle — well, maybe just a little for show. Tell her it's for two men, and that I'm at work and will be in later. I should be able to avoid her for a day or so."

A half-hour later, I heard a tapping on the window above me. It was Leon, motioning me to the front door. It turned out to be far cleaner than the last place. The couch actually looked comfortable, and I stretched out on it.

"How did she seem?"

"She's a he," Leon said. "And I think he was kind of sweet on me. You should have seen his face fall when I told him about you."

"Well, you have been in a drought."

"I'll pass, thanks. Besides the whole penis thing, he's about 70."

"You think he'll be a problem for us?"

"No," Leon said. "I didn't haggle at all. In the end, he was happy with the stack of currency."

We split a can of peaches and took a nap and just hung around. I left the flat after dark, at about 7 o'clock, to make the walk to the amphitheater. I stuck to the smallest streets, and varied the route, and came up on Raymond from a different direction than the previous times, no walk up the middle aisle of the theater. He was startled. But in the few steps I took before he saw me, it was clear that he was downcast.

"What? Tell me," I said.

"She wasn't there."

"Fuck. Fuck. Fuck."

"She wasn't at the house. She wasn't at the silk factory. Then I went to Montluc," he said. "I took some clothes and some food. I brought it to that window. You know what I'm talking about, the place where you knock and—"

"Yeah, I've been there."

"And my other dipshit cousin, Charles, you know—"

"Yeah, yeah. What?"

"She's there," Raymond said. "She got there early this morning."

"Did Charles know anything else?"

"No. Didn't know if she'd been transported to Avenue Berthelot. Didn't know anything, other than that they put her in a cell by herself. I guess that's good."

I had no idea if it was good or bad. There weren't many women in Montluc although there were some. She was way tougher than I was, but I was still sick to my stomach at the thought of her sleeping on one of those nasty straw mattresses, the insects dive-bombing her in the dark. I was mad at myself for getting her into this, but I was mad at her, too, for encouraging me. One of us, me or her or Leon, should have seen the potential danger and had her go into hiding before I pulled the trigger on Vogl. Fuck. It was just stupid.

"Look, it's not your fault," Raymond said.

"Of course it's my fucking fault."

"You might not believe it, but it's just bad luck. If you kill him, there's no problem. If you miss him and get caught, you're screwed but Manon is fine. This was the only way she could be in jeopardy — you don't kill him, you get away, and he identifies you."

"We still should have seen it—"

"You need to stop this," Raymond said. "There's a chance they might just let her go."

"You don't really believe that."

"They might."

"No, they won't," I said. "She's the only leverage they have against me, and they know it. No, they're going to keep her."

But what would they do with her? I couldn't even begin to let my mind go there. I had a brief flash of memory, of the fourth floor, but I had to avoid it. I did it by literally yelling at myself. I muttered, "Focus, goddammit," and didn't realize I had said the words out loud until Raymond said, "What?"

"I don't know."

"Whatever you're planning, I'm in," he said.

"You can't do that—"

"The hell I can't."

"No. I mean, think—"

"I'm in," he said. "I wouldn't do it for you, asshole, but I'd do anything for her."

"But what about Marie and the kids?"

"I'm not telling Marie because if I did, she'd insist on helping, too. It's family. It's France. Don't you get it by now?"

I didn't know what to say. I was more involved in the Resistance than 98 percent of Frenchmen, but I still didn't feel it the same way they did. I was anti-Nazi to the core, but they were different. They were pro-France more than anti-Nazi, and it was not a distinction without a difference. It would always be what separated me from them. And suddenly, all I could hear was what Manon was telling me the other day at the silk factory, those three words, as definitive as they were matter of fact. Three words: "I don't run."

I shook, just hearing her in my head. But I snapped back into the present pretty quickly. *Focus, goddammit.* After a minute, I told Raymond I would need at least a day to plan.

"Watch the lamppost," I said. "But even if there's nothing there, the day after tomorrow, you need to meet me at 8. Is that okay." I gave him the address of the flat Leon and I had just rented.

He said he would be there. As I was turning to leave, Raymond grabbed me and hugged me. I suddenly felt as if maybe, with him and Leon and me, that there might be a chance.

And then he whispered in my ear, "Vive la France, asshole."

47

I t was a few minutes past the curfew when I got home, mostly because I needed to duck behind a row of hedges when I saw some headlights approaching soon after I had left the amphitheater. I didn't know if it was the Gestapo or not, but there was no sense taking any chances. And besides, after talking to Raymond and getting his support, I really was feeling better. I just sat in the shrubs and relaxed until I was sure it was safe.

When I got back to the flat, the conversation with Leon was more excited than morose. The more I thought about a potential plan, the more I liked it. It was never going to be a sure thing, but it didn't feel as if it was going to be the longest shot on the board, either.

"So what are you thinking?" Leon said.

"We take her during the transport from Montluc to Avenue Berthelot," I said. "To me, it's the only way."

I told him about how it worked, about how the prisoners were chained into the back of an open lorry. I told him about how the driver and guard were both Frenchmen, not Germans, and how they always took the same long, slow, stupid route to Gestapo headquarters.

"They're not true believers," I said, referring to the driver and the guard. "They don't act like they give a shit about anything, and they show no interest at all in getting the prisoners to headquarters in a hurry. They're just working for a paycheck."

"You sure?"

"I've seen the look before," I said. "Trust me, they don't give a fuck. Being on the truck is like being on vacation for them, just a few minutes away from their foreign bosses. And if they can go extra slow, it's even a few more minutes than that. I'd just bribe them if I thought we could get away with it, because they are most definitely the bribable type."

"So if you don't bribe them?" Leon said.

"We're going to have to shoot them," I said. It was blunt, matter of fact, spoken without emotion. Leon didn't respond — not with a word, or a nod, or anything.

"I'm still working out all of the details in my head," I said. "But I have gotten that far. We're going to have to shoot the guards."

"You got a part for me in this?" Leon said.

"Are you sure?"

"I told you before, I'm sure."

"Then I think I do," I said. "I'm still thinking about a couple of different variations, but I do have a part for you, yes. And it won't involve you shooting anybody, or even carrying a gun."

"Can you tell me yet?"

"No, no details, not yet. I want to think it through for a while longer. I'm also going to need some help, hopefully from the Resistance. I can't know about that until tomorrow, and until I know if they can help, I can't really make the plan. So just be patient, okay?"

I didn't know who I was to talk, though, because patience was my biggest problem in all of this. I wanted to go right now, the next morning, but that just wasn't conceivable. I thought about what they might be doing to Manon, but it just couldn't happen that fast. To go in too quickly with a half-formed plan would be suicide for everyone. Besides, the next morning would be Sunday morning, and there was no telling what kind of schedule the Gestapo kept on the Sabbath. For all I knew, the fucking monsters all went to church, then had a nice Sunday dinner and took a day of rest. The reality was that they were all probably working overtime, searching for me — but maybe not. There just wasn't any way to know.

But how long could Manon hold out? Forget the potential for torture — with just the stress, how would it affect the pregnancy? Of course, "forget the potential for torture" was just a bunch of words. The torture was all I thought about — the bathtubs, the loppers hanging on the wall, Barbie extra nasty because his dog was dead. My mind drifted there constantly, and I had to keep dragging it back to the reality of the present. *Focus, goddammit.* Anyway, the worry must have been plain on my face.

"She'll be okay for another day," Leon said.

"I keep telling myself that, but—"

"She's fucking tougher than you — we both know that, right?"

"Three times tougher," I said.

"She'll be all right. As for you, make your plan, do it fast but do it right. You're only going to get one shot."

Leon was more than correct there. But I still had to find a way to get the plan in motion on Monday morning.

48

Marcel didn't open his shop on Sundays, but I knew he lived upstairs and I didn't have a choice. So, dressed one more time as a priest, I began knocking as loudly as I could on the front door at a little after 10 a.m. A man called out from across the street.

"Shop's closed on Sunday, Father."

"I know. But I left a gift here that I need to pick up," I said.

"Shouldn't you be in church?" The man chuckled as he said it.

"The pastor gave me the early Mass," I said. "I need to pick up the gift for my nephew's birthday."

"Well, he's closed."

"No, I'm open." I turned and saw Marcel, standing in the open doorway, wearing a nightshirt. He waved at the guy across the street as the man walked away. Then he looked at me and said, "It's not as if a person could hope to sleep late on Sunday."

"Shouldn't you be in church?" I said.

"Fuck you, Father. You coming in or not?"

He locked the door behind us. The sign in the window still

said "CLOSED". He took me to the back of the store, where he had a single gas burner, a pot and a sink. "Coffee?" he said.

"Real coffee?"

"I can't drink the fake shit."

"But where do you get it?"

"I have other talents besides forgery," he said, measuring out the water and then spooning the coffee into the filter part. Just the smell when he opened the bag of coffee brought me close to orgasm. He set the pot on the ring and lit the gas.

And then Marcel looked at me and said, "A lot of people have more than one talent. Like you, apparently."

"Don't believe everything you read."

"Why, isn't it true?"

"Well, I didn't say that."

As the coffee brewed, I told him about what happened on Friday morning. I gave him a taste of my history with Vogl, and then explained exactly why I needed to kill him, about how it would benefit me in more than one way, eliminating Vogl and perhaps putting me back in the Resistance's good graces.

"My friend said the English have a saying for it—"

"Killing two birds with one stone."

"You've heard it?" I said. "I was really liking that saying—"

"Until you didn't kill the first bird," Marcel said.

"Yeah, that," I said.

"You might have missed the Gestapo officer — what's his name? Vogl? — but you were right about the Resistance."

"Wait. What?"

"You were right about the Resistance," he said. "They're not after you anymore."

Marcel said that he knew about the shooting before it was even in the newspaper on Friday afternoon, that someone from Liberation told him at the cafe down the street when he was getting a coffee about 10:30 in the morning. And they had a meeting on Saturday morning — yesterday morning — to talk about it.

"You know, the whole Resistance council," he said.

"Were you there?"

"I didn't need to be," he said. "I have my sources. Look at this face — people just want to tell me stuff. They can't help themselves."

The coffee was ready, and Marcel poured us each a cup. It smelled so good that the aroma left me in something approaching a trance. But it was transitory. The news that Marcel was delivering was just too good to be distracted for long.

"They talked about you, the council did," he said. "It wasn't an argument, because to be honest, you didn't have any great backers in the room. But there was a general agreement that they had been wrong to doubt you, and they said you were no longer a target."

"My God," I said.

"I know," Marcel said. "If only Vogl had fucking died, your plan would have worked perfectly."

"A big if."

"The biggest."

As we drank the coffee, I explained to Marcel about Manon being taken to the prison. I started to beat myself up, and he stopped me even quicker than Raymond did.

"Look, that kind of thinking gets you nowhere," he said. "That's the kind of thinking that leads to defeat — it leads there automatically. If you think like that, you'll never get her back."

"You're right, I know. But—"

"No buts," he said. "So what's your plan?"

I sketched out the basics. He nodded but didn't offer anything in reply.

"I could use some Resistance help," I said.

"Manpower?"

"No, I don't think so. I'm pretty sure I'll have that part covered. But a gun for sure, and maybe some other stuff. You think they'll help?"

"I'll make them help," he said. I just looked at him, my face asking the question that required no words.

"Look," he said. "They all come and talk to me because they need my services. But they all come separately, and they tell me what's happening, and they bitch a little about the other groups. I hear them out. I give them advice. They listen to me — what can I say? They've already listened to me about you."

"What do you mean already?"

"When I said you didn't have any great allies in the room, I wasn't lying. But I've been advocating for you for weeks. Even before this all happened, they were starting to come around."

"You told them about smuggling the Jews?"

"Yeah," he said. "I mean, I lied some. I said I hadn't seen you in weeks. But spending your own money, running those risks for Jews on the run, it is a pretty powerful example of where your heart is."

I didn't know what to say. It might have been the nicest thing anyone had ever said about me. Part of me wanted to admit to him how reluctant I had been, how Leon and Manon were so much more sure than I was about helping the Jews, but why? *Focus, goddammit.*

"Can you set up a meeting?" I said.

"When?"

"Um, now."

"Let me get dressed," Marcel said. I poured myself another cup of coffee and thought some more about how things finally seemed to be breaking my way. Maybe, just maybe...

Ten minutes later, Marcel was cleaned up and pointing me out the back door. "To the car," he said.

"You have petrol? You have petrol and coffee?"

"Like I said, I'm multi-talented," he said. "Now lie down on the floor in the back, Father, and let me cover you with a blanket."

We drove for about 15 minutes. When we parked and Marcel told me to get up, I was looking at a part of Lyon that I was pretty sure I had never seen. There was nothing foreign or odd about it — it was just a neighborhood I didn't recognize.

"Come on," he said. We walked a half-block to a cafe on the corner.

"You're sure they're here? Did you call or anything?"

"No need. Sunday after church, they all wander over here. It's an unofficial weekly meeting."

"I don't think Manon ever came to these."

"She wasn't invited," he said. "This is just the heads of the big groups. They say they need to coordinate things for the upcoming week, and that it isn't just an excuse to get out of the house and do some day drinking, but—"

"Two birds with one stone?" I said.

"Exactly." Marcel opened the door and we walked into something called the Cafe Lafayette. We breezed through the main dining room and toward a back room whose door was closed. Marcel knocked and waited for a reply before opening the door.

49

Marcel walked in first, me behind him. There was no reaction to his entrance from the three men sitting around the big round table. Then, after a short delay, no more than a second, there was a scraping of chairs on the scarred wood floor, and a hurried rising to their feet, and a soft cacophony of mumbled good-morning-Fathers.

"And good morning to you, too," I said. Then I slowly removed the big black hat, and then the black-rimmed eyeglasses, and watched them hesitate for a second. Then the guy from *Combat* said, "My God, it's perfect."

The guy from *Liberation* said, "But didn't you wear a street sweeper's outfit when you did it?"

"I did. But I changed into this in an alley. It's pretty good, isn't it? I almost feel like I'm bulletproof when I'm wearing it."

They poured a drink for Marcel and me. We toasted to the liberation of France, which was fairly standard. They all seemed comfortable enough with my presence, but I wanted more than an unstated welcome. I wanted an apology. I knew that I needed their help, and I knew that I had already won, in the sense that I had demonstrated my loyalty and that they recognized it. But I still wanted somebody to say it.

So I drank and didn't say a word. I took a sip and put the glass back on the table, and I just sat there. The three of them looked at Marcel, and then at each other, but nobody said anything. So I took another sip, and set the glass down again, and put on as placid and as blank a face as I could manage. I wanted to fold my arms in defiance, but I resisted. I wanted to sneer at them, to scream at them, to yell just two words at them: "Well, motherfuckers..." But I just sat there.

Marcel knew what I was waiting for. We made just the quickest bit of eye contact, and I could tell. And eventually, after about 90 very uncomfortable seconds, after a long stare in his direction from Marcel, the guy from *Le Franc-Tireur* cleared his throat.

"Allain, Alex, whatever, you must understand," he said.

"Understand what?"

"You know what we were looking at." It was the guy from *Liberation*. "You know how men were being captured—"

"And you know I had proved my loyalty a dozen times over."

"You must be reasonable." It was the guy from *Combat* now. They were all taking a turn. "The pressure—"

"Fuck that. You never even asked. You just shot."

"And we were wrong," Le Franc-Tireur said. "You deserved better." He refilled everyone's glass and offered a toast.

"To the future," he said. As Marcel eyed me carefully and sternly, I replied, "To the future," right along with the rest of them. I dodged a couple of bullets, they offered a short apology — it didn't exactly seem equitable. But it wasn't nothing, and it was the best I was going to do. Besides, I still needed their assistance. So, to the future.

The three of them, publishers of the three biggest Resistance newspapers, leaders of the three biggest sub-groups within the organization, wanted to hear all about how little old me managed to shoot Vogl all by myself. I gave them the full version, from my meal with Vogl in the bouchon to me walking over Pont Gallieni and looking back over my shoulder to see the Gestapo running out of Avenue Berthelot toward Vogl's body.

"Vogl was right, we saw you in the bouchon," said the Liberation guy. "We saw you inside, and we saw the hug on the sidewalk when you were leaving."

"I can only imagine what you thought," I said. No one offered a reply. To the future. *Focus, goddammit.*

"We have a guy in the hospital, an orderly on Vogl's floor," said the guy from *Combat*. "Unfortunately for you, he says that they're pretty sure Vogl is going to live. And he's not paralyzed — although it isn't as if he's walking around, either. But he can't talk, and they don't know if he's going to be able to again. He communicates everything by writing it down."

There was a knock at the door. When it opened, a man in an apron poked in his head and said, "Black Citroen just drove by."

"Things have really heated up since you shot him," said the guy from *Combat*.

"For me," I said.

"For all of us, especially since they took Manon," said the guy from *Le Franc-Tireur*.

"So you know?"

"We know everything," said the *Liberation* guy. His delivery was deadpan. There was not the hint of a smile or of irony. If he knew what an ass he sounded like, he didn't let on. *Yeah, you know fucking everything, except for who the truly loyal people are.* But I had to let that go.

"Will you help me?" I said.

"We have some ideas.," the *Liberation* guy said.

"So do I."

I started by talking in generalities. I said, "I think our best chance to get her, really our only chance, is during the transfer from Montluc to Avenue Berthelot."

The three of them all looked at each other and nodded. It was me and them, with Marcel as an impassive observer.

"We have talked and we agree about the transfer being the best opportunity," the guy from *Combat* said. But as he and the others spoke more, there was a disagreement about what each of us thought was best.

They favored an attempt to grab her right outside the gates of Montluc when the prisoners were being loaded into the lorry. It happened out in the open, right on the sidewalk, in plain sight. They didn't even do anything special to prevent a pedestrian from walking by when the transfer was happening.

"It's wide open," the *Le Franc-Tireur* guy said. "It's at 9 o'clock every morning. We've watched it from a distance, probably a dozen times in the last six months. It's always the same, always wide open, always at 9 o'clock."

I understood what they were saying, and I had considered it, but I didn't like it — mostly because of the Gestapo. When the prison was run entirely by French guards, maybe — but even then, the first shot would have brought guards swarming out of the front gate, and while they might have been sleepy mercenaries, they still had guns. Now, though, the guards rushing out at the sound of the gunshot would be wearing black uniforms.

"It's just too dangerous," I said, and then I started to explain my plan to them. At one point, in order to show what I was talking about, I asked if they had a map of the city. The *Liberation* guy replied with a look that I interpreted as his do-we-have-a-fucking-map look, and then he stood up, and reached out his arms about as wide as they would go, and lifted an enormous charcoal drawing of the entrance to a Paris metro station from the wall and placed it between us on the table. A detailed street map of Lyon was on the back side.

We all stood up and I began to trace the route that the transport took between Montluc and Avenue Berthelot. They all looked at me like I was crazy.

"I'm telling you — I rode it three times and it was the exact same way all three times," I said.

"But—"

"It's—"

"I know, it makes no sense," I said, and then went on to spout my theory about how they were just trying to prolong their time away from their Gestapo bosses.

"But what if they go a different way?"

"I have that covered," I said. "And if I'm wrong, we'll do it your way on Tuesday."

They all looked at each other, heads shaking back and forth.

"You want to do this *tomorrow*?" the *Combat* guy said. He checked his wristwatch. "Like, 18 hours from now?"

They all looked at each other again, seemingly uncertain. But then the guy from *Liberation* shrugged theatrically and said, "What the hell. Okay, what do you need? How many men?"

"I don't need men," I said. "I have some help, and I honestly believe that fewer men will be better."

I explained what I needed. They said it would not be a problem. We talked about the mechanics a little more. Then we drank another toast — again, to the future.

50

Marcel said he would drive me back to the flat. I wanted to sit next to him in the front seat and enjoy the ride. He insisted I go back onto the floor of the back seat, again beneath the blanket.

I objected and said, "It's a good disguise. I'm willing to risk it. It's my ass on the line."

He just looked at me, and shook his head, and said, "Self-absorbed much, are you?"

So I went beneath the blanket. We were at the flat in about 20 minutes. Marcel parked, and we both were standing on the sidewalk, when he flipped me the keys. Surprised, I fumbled them and then dropped them.

"What's this?" I said.

"I listened to everything you told the council," he said. "And I think you're probably going to need another vehicle. You might need it in the morning. You might need it later. But I think you're probably going to need it."

"But—"

"Shut up," Marcel said. "There's about a half-tank of petrol left. There are two full jerry cans in the trunk. If I had to guess, you could go about 150 miles with all of that, maybe closer to 200."

"But—"

"Again, shut up. You're going to need options pretty soon, whether the rescue works or not. If you get her, you and Manon and probably Leon are going to have to hide somewhere for a while. If you don't get her, you're going to need to fucking run."

"I'm not running without her."

"You say that now," he said. "But suicide doesn't become you. You'll need to survive if you're ever going to have a chance to save her. And this will give you another option."

"I don't know what to say."

"Just fucking say thank you," Marcel said. We hugged and whispered simultaneously, "Vive la France." I'm not sure I had ever said it before on my own, without prompting. Before that, it had always been as a polite reply to someone else.

He walked away, then stopped and turned. "Oh yeah," he said. "If you get a chance, drop me a note at the shop to tell me where you leave it. Oh, and don't think I forgot that you didn't buy a stamp after your last visit."

"But the last one I bought was shit."

"Don't I know it," he said. "Don't I know it."

When I got inside the flat, Raymond was already there with Leon. They were drinking from a fairly full bottle of Calvados. I held it up and whistled in appreciation.

"We keep it for special occasions, but Marie made me take it," Raymond said. "It being a special occasion and all."

"I thought you weren't going to tell her."

"I had to," he said. "And I was right — she wanted to help. And I actually thought of a way."

"But you don't even know the plan yet," I said.

"I know. But you tell me, and then I'll tell you if it makes sense."

My original thought was that Raymond would have to be in uniform and "requisition" a vehicle from the police station in order to play his part. But now, with Marcel's generosity, there was another option: Raymond could be in civilian clothes and drive Marcel's car instead. We debated back and forth because there were pluses and minuses to each version. In the end, we decided on Marcel's car and civilian clothes.

I didn't have a city map, so I had to draw the key streets freehand on a tablet. I was pretty close to having it exactly correct, and certainly close enough — because Leon would have plenty of time to get in position, even if he got a little bit lost initially, and because Raymond had been posted all over the city during his career as a cop and knew the neighborhood pretty well already.

We went over the plan several times, and the truth was that it sounded more and more plausible as the bottle of Calvados grew emptier and emptier. After a while, the three of us settled into long silences that were broken only by the sound of refilling glasses and random questions.

"What about the lorry?" Leon said.

"They're bringing it," I said. "Right to the curb out front. Sometime during the night. And the gun will be in the glove box, a pistol with at least four bullets. It seems like the bullets are the hardest part."

"And what about the other prisoners?" Raymond said.

"We let them go, and hope they run like hell," I said. "It's a risk if they get caught, and I know that. But if they do, we can only hope that they have shitty memories for faces."

We turned out the lights at 10, so as not to draw attention to ourselves on a dark, quiet block, where everyone was likely trying to sleep before work on Monday morning. We kept our voices low. The random questions became less frequent. At around midnight, we all heard a vehicle park in front and the slam of a door. I peeked out from behind the curtain, and it was the lorry, as promised.

"Wait," I said. "What was your plan for Marie?"

"Oh, right," Raymond said, and he told us.

"But I thought—"

"Alex, think about it," he said. "This is better."

"I don't know."

We fell asleep undecided.

51

W e all slept until sunrise, despite our nerves; God bless Calvados. Until about 7:30, we went over the plan a few more times until each of us could repeat the details flawlessly. We even synchronized our watches, mostly because it made sense but partly because it was something Raymond once saw in a movie.

We would leave the flat separately, not so much for any security reasons but because of the realities of our travel schedules. I would leave first, at about 8, because I was walking. Then Raymond would leave at about 8:15 because he needed to drive out of the way to pick up Marie before going to the prison. Leon would leave last, at about 8:30, because his was the straightest and shortest route.

One more time, I dusted off my old friends for duty — the cassock, the wide-brimmed black hat, and the breviary. I wondered if this would be the last day I wore them. It wasn't a meditation on my own mortality, although I was about to put that mortality to a pretty severe test. It was mostly a law of averages calculation. The disguise had been so good to me, for so long and in so many situations, but how much longer could that possibly continue? How much longer before they compared enough eyewitness reports of a priest following Vogl on his route to Avenue Berthelot, and another priest gawking at his fallen body, and now another priest leaving the scene of the lorry hijacking, before some star pupil in a black uniform figured it was just one too many priests in wide-brimmed hats for it to be a coincidence?

Still, the disguise would have to serve me this one last day. I pulled on the cassock over my regular clothes, which included an added accessory: the pistol jammed into the waist of my pants. It had five bullets, one more than promised. It was my lucky day, although I was hoping to get away with firing only two.

I was oddly calm on the walk over. I knew I would be shitting myself in the moment, but for some reason, I felt great during the buildup. I just kept reciting the details, again and again and again.

Raymond would arrive at Montluc at 8:55. He was to park on the same street as the main gate, but a block away. When he stopped the car, he would pull up the hood as if there was a problem with the engine. He would take off his coat, and roll up his sleeves, and remove the tool kit from the trunk and begin tinkering. If anyone happened by and had a question, or offered help, he would say that it looked like one of the wires had come loose from the battery somehow, and that he would tighten it and be on his way. Marie would be waiting inside the car, reading a newspaper. Raymond had won that argument.

Raymond's job was simple: to be in a position to see whether Manon was loaded onto the lorry with the rest of the prisoners. If she was, the original plan was for him just to drive away, his part completed. Now, though, if Manon was on the lorry, Raymond and Marie were supposed to follow the lorry on its journey, but not closely. They should stay at least a block behind, and maybe more.

But if Manon was not among the load of prisoners, Raymond needed to speed up and do everything he could to get in front of the lorry, blowing his horn loudly and angrily and often enough so that Leon and I would hear, several blocks ahead. A persistent horn was the signal to abort the mission. This was the part where a police car would have been a better option because of the siren. The downside was that Lyon police cars had identifying numbers, and Raymond would have been at more of a risk if someone remembered the number. All in all, this would work better — provided he really leaned on the horn.

As I made my way, the sidewalk began to fill with the people of Lyon, people heading to their jobs. No one gave me a second look. They all had their own problems, most of which involved finding enough to eat. It was the constant in Lyon and all over France. Pretty much every day, you went to work hungry. And pretty much every night, you left work and attempted to scrounge up some dinner. There were always two questions — how many coupons do I have left, and will the store have anything to buy except those goddamn Jerusalem artichokes?

That day, I felt privileged because I didn't feel particularly hungry, mostly because I did feel slightly hungover. It was as if the hangover was a welcome distraction, not that it kept me from running the plan through my head in a continuous loop.

While Raymond was setting up at the prison, Leon was to drive the small lorry provided by the Resistance to Rue Saint-Hippolyte and wait at the corner where it intersected with Petite Rue de Montplaisir. The street was, as the named suggested, petite. For the lorry containing the prisoners, it was quite snug. If the driver could manage 20 miles an hour, it would be an accomplishment. It was much more likely he'd be doing 15, and maybe 10. It was the most insane stretch of the entirely insane route. If Leon was parked right at the corner, he would have no trouble seeing the lorry slowly maneuvering down the tiny street and pulling in front of it to block its path.

As I walked, there were enough people on the streets that I began to get worried. Leon would be parked about 150 feet from a relatively busy street. What were the odds, just after 9, that no bystander would happen upon the operation? It was tough to know. If we were quick enough, it wouldn't be a problem. If we were unlucky, it would be the same risk as with the other prisoners. All we could do was hope they didn't get a good look at any of our faces. There really wasn't a choice because this was the best spot and we had no control over the timing.

So, at maybe five minutes past 9, Leon would pull out in front of the lorry, blocking its path. Then he would act as if he stalled out when trying to shift into reverse and was stuck, which wouldn't be hard because Leon couldn't drive for shit. But even if it was an act, it wouldn't have to be for long.

Because while all of that was happening, I would step out from the alley that separated two of the buildings on Petite Rue de Montplaisir and do what I needed to do. One shot, two shots, fin. And then we would grab the keys from the guard, unlock Manon and the rest of the prisoners, and make our escape. Leon would take the truck alone. Manon would get in the car with Raymond and Marie, which was just pulling up from behind and parked, about 100 feet back, and ready to avoid the bottleneck by making a left turn onto Rue de la Promenade.

And I would walk back into the alley, pull the cassock over my head, push the black hat down low, pick up my breviary, and walk out of the other side of the alley a little farther down onto Rue Saint-Hippolyte.

52

I turned left onto Petite Rue de Montplaisir. My period of calm had passed, and the needle on the dial, which featured a scale from Zero to Shitting Myself, was moving persistently to the right. As I turned, I gave a quick peek over my shoulder, which was bad spy craft — but I didn't care. I needed the reassurance that nobody was following me as I turned onto the quiet, narrow street, and nobody was.

I got a second look about 15 seconds later when I crossed the street and made the right-hand turn onto Rue Saint-Hippolyte. I was gloriously clean, and there was no one on the street ahead of me, either. After another 15 seconds, I ducked into the alley that formed two sides of the perimeter of the building that sat on the corner. I would walk in one side, on Rue Saint-Hippolyte, make the left at the alley's deepest point, and then come out on Petite Rue de Montplaisir.

There were some big trash bins, and it was behind them that I removed the cassock and the hat, leaving me in ordinary work clothes. I checked my watch, and it was five minutes before nine. If the mission was to be aborted because Manon was not on the lorry, Raymond would theoretically begin blasting his car horn in five minutes. If there was no horn, the lorry from Montluc would be in front of me about five minutes after that.

I wanted to venture out to the end of the alley to take a quick peek and see if Leon was in position with the lorry that the Resistance had provided. I actually took a step in that direction and then stopped myself. What was the point? None, actually. If Leon wasn't there, I would know soon enough — because the lorry from the prison would drive right by me if he wasn't there. If he was there, the lorry would be stopped and I would do what I had to do. But to go out and look would just be to risk giving my position away to some bystander who happened upon the scene. There was no need for that. In fact, it was stupid even to have considered it.

I looked again at my watch. Two minutes before nine. My hands were shaking but only a little bit. I was actually surprised that my fear was not showing worse — because it was intense. The only way I could distract myself was to think about Manon. Of course, every time I did that, my mind would wander to the worst. At one point, I actually imagined what her left hand would look like with her pinky lopped off. Would I even notice if she wasn't wearing her wedding ring anymore? A second after that gruesome sight filled my mind's eye, I managed a *focus, goddammit* that I verbalized loud enough that I felt as if it might have echoed in the closed space.

My watch, again. It was 9 o'clock.

I crept out toward the entrance of the alley on Petite Rue de Montplaisir. I needed to stick my head out, at least a little, to listen for a blaring car horn, first in the distance and then growing louder. But there was nothing. I cocked my ear to the right, in the direction of the prison — and, nothing. But then I thought I heard something coming from the left. I looked, and the first thing I saw was Leon in his truck, sitting on the corner of Rue Saint-Hippolyte. So that was good. But what was the noise? I was pretty sure that it was a train blowing its horn, but the tracks were easily a mile away. Was it crazy that I could hear it? And was it really to the left, or was it a noise coming from the right and the sound waves were ricocheting off of a building?

Steady, steady. *Focus, goddammit.* I closed my eyes and tried to concentrate some more on any sounds coming from my right, from the direction of Montluc. But there was nothing.

My watch. It was 9:03, and all was quiet. This was really happening. I looked quickly at Leon, and from 100 or so feet away, our eyes still managed to meet. We traded a nod. Yes, this was really happening.

I stepped back into the alley to wait. Maybe two minutes later, maybe three, it all began to unfold. I could feel my heart in my chest but, at the same time, it felt as if everything was happening in slow motion. I felt like I was underwater.

The lorry from Montluc rumbled slowly down the street, its exhaust farting once in exasperation at the slow speed. Leon pulled out exactly as planned, and the prison lorry stopped. The driver threw his hands in the air as if outraged by the delay. Leon waved back in what appeared to be a sincere apology. Then he struggled to get the lorry into reverse and put on a very convincing show of looking very much like a new driver who was choking under the pressure.

That's when I came out of the alley.

My thought all along had been to shoot the guard first and the driver second. The risk was that the driver would floor it in response to the shot and turn a relatively controlled situation for me into a total fucking mess. But the risk the other way was just as plain. I wasn't sure that the driver was armed, but I knew the guard was — so shooting the driver first would give the guard more time to get to his weapon. I debated it, and even adding in that the driver would be closest to me as I approached the lorry, I still thought it made sense to shoot the guard first. And so I did.

One shot to the head. The driver did not floor it — he simply froze. He got the second bullet, also to the head. One, two. I felt nothing, other than relief. They were two Frenchmen, just working for a living, maybe true Nazi believers but more likely just a couple of saps who couldn't think of another way to feed their families. It could have been Raymond if he had been a prison guard before the war instead of a city cop. But I really didn't care. One, two.

Leon jumped out of his lorry and ran to get the keys from the dead guard's pocket. I reflexively wiped the gun off on my shirt-tail and dropped it down a sewer on the corner. I didn't really care if the Gestapo found the gun or not. Honestly, my first thought was to take the remaining three bullets out of the revolver so I could give them back to the Resistance.

I wanted to see Manon, to hug her, hold her, console her — but if everyone was unanimous about one aspect of the plan, it was that I was to go nowhere near the back of the lorry when Leon was unlocking the chains. The *Combat* guy was the first one to say, "You can't do it. If the other prisoners connect the two of you, and one of them gets caught, they'll focus on you as the culprit. This way, they'll have to guess for a little while, at least. They'll see it as a Resistance operation, not an Alex operation. They still think we're after you. You want that confusion. It probably won't last, but even a little while will help."

So I stood and watched from 150 feet away as the unlocked prisoners began running, five of them in five different directions. The sixth was Manon, who did not run. She walked quickly in the direction of Marcel's car, where Raymond was leaning out of the driver's side window and waving.

When she got there, she reached for the handle and looked in my direction for some reason. It was total happenstance. But she saw me, and our eyes locked. She stopped for just a second, stopped and placed her right hand over her heart. I did the same thing in reply.

53

Cassock on, wide-brimmed hat in place, breviary in hand, I walked out of the alley on Rue Saint-Hippolyte and turned left, away from Petite Rue de Montplaisir. I took the quickest of looks to my right and saw that Leon's lorry was gone. Just the nose of the Montluc lorry was visible to me during my peek. I couldn't see either of the bodies, and I didn't hear any police sirens. I also didn't see any bystanders. If you didn't witness what had happened, there really wasn't anything particularly compelling about the scene. The guard and the driver were both dead, but they were still in their seats in the front cab of the lorry. The prisoners were gone, but there was nothing noteworthy about an empty lorry. And the fact that it was stopped in the middle of a tiny street would draw no natural attention, either, not until a driver came up from behind and couldn't get through and began leaning on his horn. But that hadn't happened yet.

It had all gone so well that it almost beat the natural pessimism out of me. Almost.

My next task was simple, just to walk back to the flat. That was where Leon, Raymond and I all would meet up to plan for the next steps. I didn't know who would get there first. My walk would be side streets and small streets, maybe just a little bit windier than a typical walk. Leon, meanwhile, had to drop off the lorry in the back of a warehouse, leaving the keys in the ignition, and then he was to walk the rest of the way, maybe a half-mile.

Then there was Raymond. This was the part I argued against, but eventually relented. Since none of us knew what kind of physical shape Manon would be in — Manon and the baby, rather — the thought was that she needed to see someone with some medical knowledge as soon as possible after the rescue. That was where Marie's idea came into play. I was being selfish — I just wanted to see my wife — but the logic of her argument eventually wore me down.

Because, as it turned out, Marie made a little money on the side by doing laundry for the nuns at the convent of the Church of Saint Bruno des Chartreaux. With that job came two interesting side benefits. First, she would have access to nuns' habits — dress, veil, the whole deal. Second, she had a relationship with Sister Jerome, who was a trained nurse and a Resistance sympathizer at the same time. All of which meant that, waiting in the back seat of the car lent to us by Marcel were two nuns' habits, which Manon and Marie slipped into while Raymond drove back toward the convent. Once there, Raymond would let them out about a block away and they would walk into the front door of the convent as any two nuns might — and, once inside, Sister Jerome would give Manon as much of a physical examination as her abilities allowed. Raymond had said, "She's good — she was a full-time nurse before she received the calling." So if Manon and/or the baby were in significant distress, we would know and could plan on a next move.

Me walking in a cassock. Manon dressed up like a nun and

hiding out in a convent. The two of us really were going to have to get our asses into a church pretty soon.

I got back to the flat first, then Leon. Raymond was last, which surprised me. He said there was no particular reason. He just drove slowly, in a little bit of a circuitous route. "It's like I'm in a fucking daze," he said. "It's like I can't believe it. I mean, are we really going to get away with this?"

"How is she?" I said.

"She's good," Raymond said.

"Good how?"

"She's tired, but that's it. She said they never beat her, never really touched her."

"Ten fingers and toes?" I said.

"Ten and ten," he said. "I didn't see any bloody stumps. She said they kept her up all night at Montluc — lights bright, guards coming by to wake her every 15 minutes. At Avenue Berthelot, she said Barbie—"

"Barbie himself?" I said.

"The man himself, in the flesh. She said he asked where you were, if you shot at Vogl. She said she hadn't seen you in weeks. He asked again, she said the same thing. Eight hours of questioning on Saturday, then no sleep, then eight more hours of questioning on Sunday, then no sleep. But she's okay."

"Did she say anything about the baby?"

"She did," Raymond said. "Marie asked her straight off and Manon said, 'He's a kicking bastard.' She thinks it's a boy, because he's such an asshole."

She had never guessed at the sex before. I sank back into the couch cushion and just about passed out. And then I said, "I know what you mean about the daze. It's almost like it went too well."

"Don't celebrate too soon," Leon said. "We still haven't figured out how to get you two out of here."

"I was think—" Raymond said.

"You stop thinking right now," I said. "I can't begin to thank you, and I'll never be able to pay you back for your help and your friendship. But it ends here."

"Now wait—"

"Now you fucking wait," I said. "This is it. You have Marie. You have the kids. You have a life, and you've already risked too much. So when you get home tonight, you give Marie and the kids a hug for me, and you tell her that it's over. We've been given a blessing here — nobody saw you two, and nobody suspects you of anything — and we have to accept that blessing. It's about time we got one."

Raymond folded his arms and just stared at me. He was pissed off, but he knew I was right. Leon walked over and put his arm around him and said, "Think about the stories we'll be able to tell when these motherfucking black uniforms are gone." Raymond just continued to stare. That was his reply.

We hadn't talked about what was next, but I was pretty sure that Manon and I were going to have to leave Lyon specifically, and the area in general. There just wasn't any way we could survive the manhunt that was ongoing, and that would likely be turned up even hotter now that Manon had escaped. We had to go, and we had to go soon. Manon could say all she wanted that she didn't run, but this would not be running. This would be surviving to fight another day.

Leon knew what I was thinking, and the argument that would be coming, and said, "Tell her it's just a tactical retreat."

But when would I be able to tell her? The plan was that Leon and I would hide for as long as we could and somehow get in touch with the Resistance through Marcel to find out the next move. Manon, meanwhile, would stay in the convent until the Resistance scooped her up and got us back together. The truth was, I might not be the one who made the argument to her about leaving after all. It might be someone from the Resistance. She would be livid, and I was silently hoping the messenger would be the motherfucking ass-grabber.

Whatever, we were going to have to leave the flat and get in the car and find a new place to hide out. We would have to keep moving, never spending more than one night anywhere. And we were going to have to find a way to get in touch with Marcel on a fairly regular basis. And, ideally, we would have an idea about what we were doing in a couple of days, tops.

We were getting ready to go. Raymond would go first and walk home. He had left a uniform here so that, during the walk, no one would bother him. As he buttoned up and got ready to leave, he just shook his head.

"I wish we had another bottle of Calvados," he said.

The postcard to Marcel said:

> *The trip was fantastic! Thanks so much for your hospitality! The 5th course of that late night dinner will never*

be forgotten! All our love, and next time, you must visit us.

Anthon

Marcel wasn't a spy, but we were hoping he could figure it out. The key words were "5th," "late-night" and "Anthon." What we were hoping was that Marcel would take the local train out to Anthon, a little town about 20 miles east of Lyon, on the 5th of the month, late at night, and find Leon and I sitting in his car, which would be parked just outside the station.

Which was exactly what happened.

"Thank fucking God," he said, when he saw us.

"I told you he had the makings of a spy," I said.

"You're a spy? Not just a half-assed Resistance fighter?"

"It's a long story," Leon said.

"I have time, I'm driving," Marcel said. "But talk loud."

"Why?"

"Because the two of you are laying down on the floor of the

back seat and hiding under a blanket. And don't worry — I'll give you all the privacy you need."

"But there's nobod—" I said.

"My ride, my rules," he said.

The ride was uneventful. We hadn't even had to go to the jerry cans in the trunk during the days we were hiding out. One night, we slept in the barn at Marcel Lefebvre's farm at Chassagny. He gave us homemade wine, and milk, and even poached a couple of eggs for us. I nearly cried. The next night, Leon rented a room at an inn with his most recent identity, and I sneaked in to join him. Another night, we hid behind the barn of what seemed to be an abandoned farm — maybe owned by Jews, but who knew? — and slept in the car. It hadn't been too bad at all.

"How's Manon?" I said. It was when we first stared driving.

"Good," Marcel said. "The sister said she and the baby are fine. They said she slept for the better part of two days, only getting up to eat a little. The Resistance has her in a safe house now. We're just waiting."

"Waiting for what?"

"For the radio," Marcel said. "For tonight."

When the car eventually stopped, Marcel told us to stay where we were. He got out of the car, then unlocked the back door of his shop. He waited for an unusually long time before saying, 'Okay, come on out," which we did.

"Why the wait?" I said.

"I don't know," Marcel said. "I'm losing my nerve, not that I ever had any. But this is killing me. Every time I see a black uniform, I feel like pissing myself. I know it must show on my face. I'm just waiting for the knock."

"You'll be all right," Leon said. "You've been very careful."

"But I've been more involved than I ever thought I would be," he said. "It all just... happened."

"You sorry you did it?" I said.

"No, no — it's not that. I know what I'm doing is important. I know it's the most important thing I've ever done. But I'm just so goddamned scared all the time. I'm seeing shadows that aren't there."

We went up to the second floor, above the shop, where Marcel lived in a fairly cramped flat — living room, bedroom, kitchenette, bathroom, fin. He settled us down and heated up some tomato soup from a tin that he stretched with some water. While we drank it out of mugs, he went back into a bottom cupboard and brought out a small box that looked as if it could hold a pair of shoes. But when he flipped off the lid, he did not bring out a pair of brogues. Instead it was a radio that he plugged in.

"Wow, it's tiny," Leon said.

"If they did a real search, they'd find it. A half-assed search, probably not. But if I had to move, I could easily take it with me."

"How do you get all of this stuff?" I said.

"You'd be amazed what you can get in exchange for two perfect identity cards."

Marcel flipped on the set and we waited for it to warm up. When it was ready, he would turn it to the BBC. Listening to it was a crime in itself, punishable by a visit to Avenue Berthelot at the minimum. They didn't really hurt you for that — they just did what they could to scare the piss out of you. Oh, and they took the radio. But on the list of Gestapo sins that I had committed in the previous few months, a little BBC radio broadcast was decidedly venial. Like, two Hail Marys' worth.

The way Marcel told it, the Resistance, after talking to their bosses in London, made the case that Manon and I needed to be flown to England. "Think about it," he said. "Married, with a child on the way, both been arrested, both well-known to the

Gestapo, and you being wanted for trying to kill a Gestapo officer and for killing two French prison guards."

"What?"

"Yeah, they've pinned that on you, too," he said. "It would be highly unfair of them to have made the assumption based on no evidence — highly unfair, that is, if it wasn't true."

"Well, there is that," I said.

"Anyway, the Resistance in London agreed immediately that you need to be airlifted out."

"And what did my beautiful bride have to say about that?"

"The way it was described to me was that, when she first heard the plan, she blistered everyone within range, really peeled the paint off the walls. But it was only for about five minutes. Then she calmed down. She knows. She knows how dangerous it is for you two. She knows how tired she is."

For the previous couple of days, I had actually allowed myself to think about what life might be like away from France and away from the Nazis. On and off for about five years, I had been either fighting them, or running from them, or both. And while we weren't there yet, not nearly, and there were still a dozen things that could land me back in Barbie's fourth floor recreation room at Avenue Berthelot, I was starting to hope that maybe, just maybe, it would all work out for us in the end. I couldn't remember the last time I'd held a legitimate hope for happiness in my heart. Honestly, it felt a little strange.

"So, what are we waiting to hear?" Leon said.

"You've listened before, right?" Marcel said.

"In Paris, all the time — but really just for the news."

"After the news, they read off personal messages. It can be kind of hypnotic because they read a bunch of them in random order. Some of them are legitimate — and a happy fortieth birthday to you, too, Andre — but a lot of them are coded messages to the Resistance, just sentences or phrases or quotes from literature. It's pretty simple. The details have been worked out ahead of time. We're just waiting for a go or a no-go. And a date."

The news came on, and the headlines were all about the war. The summary was that the good guys were doing swell and the Germans were losing in Russia, toe by frostbitten toe. I didn't know how much of it was true, but I was inclined to believe more than I typically did. It must have been all of that hope in my heart, I guess, or something.

I started to make a crack about the eastern front when Marcel shushed me. It was apparent that he needed to concentrate. Pencil in hand, pad of paper on the table in front of him, he was leaned over with his ear right next to the radio's speaker. He was concentrating so hard that he was squinting.

Then he began writing. When it was over, he snapped off the radio and unplugged it and began to put it back in the box.

"Well, are you going to tell us?" I said.

"The message was, 'They will leave with joy.' It's been repeated three times. What that means is, you're going out tomorrow night."

55

According to Marcel, weather and the moon had a lot to do with how they picked the dates for these flying snatches. They needed enough moonlight to be able to see the landing area, although we would help with some torches. And it had to be decent flying weather.

"The way they explained it to me, somewhat shitty is better than dead clear," Marcel said. "But, at the same time, too shitty would completely block out the moonlight."

"I'm no expert, but this night seems to be in a good place on the shittiness scale," Leon said. It had drizzled earlier, and now you could see the clouds as they moved gently across the face of a three-quarter moon.

"Prime shittiness," Marcel said.

"Enough with this shit," I said. "Where's Manon?"

We were on our bellies, behind a hedgerow. On the other side was a fallow field that didn't seem big enough to land a plane. But somebody at the Resistance had told Marcel, "Don't have a heart attack when you see it. It's small, but we've used it before."

"Manon's on the other side, behind the next hedgerow,"

Marcel said. "Don't worry. She has two people watching her, just like you have Leon and I. It's going to be fine. They do this all the time."

"All the time," I said.

"Well, they've done it before," Marcel said.

"How many times?" At this, Marcel paused.

"Twice," he said. "At least that's what they told me."

"And it worked?"

"Same answer: at least that's what they told me."

Marcel checked his watch and said, "Okay, five minutes." Then he went over the mechanics of the plan. He handed Leon a torch and told him to crab-walk down to the far end of the hedgerow. When he heard an airplane engine, he was to turn on the torch and point it straight up to the sky.

"Make sure it's straight up — don't go spraying the countryside with the light," he said. "I'll be at the other end of the hedgerow with my torch, doing the same thing. On Manon's side, there will be two more men with two more torches. The pilot will see the four lights and do his best to land in the middle of the box. The moon will help him see just enough to make it work out okay."

"And where will I be?" I said.

"You wait at the opening in the middle of the hedgerow. Manon will be in the same place on the other side. And when you see the plane land, you run for it and she'll do the same thing and, if it all works out, you'll be eating a plate of that godawful British food in no time."

"It's got to be better than what we have here," I said.

"Maybe," Marcel said. "But think about it. It takes the fucking Nazis to turn their culinary crap into something desirable."

The idea of leaving Leon behind still bothered me. I tried,

for the third time, to talk him into tagging along. He declined, for the third time, each attempt increasingly more pissed off.

"First off, I wasn't invited," he said. "But even if I was, I couldn't go. I belong here. I belong in Paris, really. Nobody's looking for me. My picture isn't on any wanted posters. I don't have a pregnant wife who just spent a couple of days in a Gestapo cell. It's just different for you."

"I know, but—"

"No buts," Leon said. "Just fucking get on the plane and send me a postcard. Maybe one with those guards in the red outfits."

Marcel checked his wristwatch again. It was time for Leon and him to get in their places. They each grabbed a torch and scuttled their way to either end of the hedgerow. I scuttled, too, the short distance to the opening. I looked through it in an attempt to see Manon, but it was too dark. I would be able to see her on the field, but the hedgerows threw enough of a shadow to leave me, and I assumed her, in a deep green darkness.

And then I just listened. I heard the faintest bit of wind in the trees behind us where the car was hidden. I did not hear an airplane engine. I counted to 60, and then I counted to 60 again, and nothing. The plane was late. I began to fidget. I needed to take a nervous piss. I wanted to crab-walk my way back over to Marcel to see what he thought, but that would be stupid. I decided on the piss instead, figuring that one of the rules of human existence would kick in. It was the same rule that said you could stand at a bus stop and lean out expectantly seemingly forever, but that the bus would not show up until you gave up and sat down on the bench.

And so, I was halfway through the piss when Leon was the first of the four to switch on his torch. I had not heard anything. But then the rest came on, and the box's four corners were lit, and the noise of the airplane grew uncomfortably loud. At a certain point, I could see it, moonlit at times, and then in the clouds, and then moonlit again. It passed over the field, and I wondered if the pilot had seen the lights, but then it banked and turned. He saw us and was just getting his nose turned back toward England as he landed.

He was coming in crazily steep, it seemed to me. Then again, I didn't know shit about flying an airplane. Still, he landed hard and bounced noticeably, once, then twice. But he had the thing under control, and was braking to a stop, much closer to Manon's hedgerow than to mine. I probably had 350 feet to run. She would have about 150 feet. That was good. She would get to the plane first and get set, and then I would dive in we would be gone.

As soon as it became clear that the brakes would hold, I began to sprint. I was maybe 10 strides into my run when the three floodlights were switched on at once. The first thing I did was stare at the lights, which were perched on the back of vehicles hidden on a hill, in another row of trees behind the other hedgerow. The second thing I did was look for Manon, and I did see her. She must have started running before me because she was nearly to the plane.

I could see her face, just for a flash, and it did not show fear, not a bit. It just showed determination, the will that defined her. It was the face I had fallen in love with.

It was the only thought I had when I heard the first gunshot, and when I felt that I had been hit in the right leg.

I fell to the ground and instinctively covered my head. I heard several more shots — rifle shots, not a machine gun. That's when I heard Manon scream.

Suddenly, amid the firing, the airplane was accelerating and gaining altitude, flying right over the lights. They must have been searchlights, employed specifically with this purpose in mind, and they followed the plane into the sky, and the shooting continued. Because of that, the field was dark again. I did my best to get to my feet, but immediately fell back down. From my back, I turned to where the plane had been, but I couldn't see anything. It was too dark. I thought I yelled Manon's name, but I wasn't sure. The only thing I was sure about was that I did not hear a reply.

I was in the process of passing out. The last thing I remembered was Marcel and Leon getting me upright and carrying me, one beneath each armpit.

56

I was in and out of consciousness for the better part of a day, I figured. I remembered bits of the ride in Marcel's car, with me stretched out on the back seat and Leon kneeling on the floor and applying pressure to my wound. The bullet caught me on the back of the thigh. At least, that's where he was pressing.

The next memory was of being stretched out, face-down, on a long table. A doctor, or whatever reasonable facsimile that the Resistance could provide, was peering into the wound while holding a flashlight. He said, to someone, "He's fainting because of the blood loss but I think he's lucky as hell. Doesn't look like anything major was hit, and there are two holes. Bullet went in one hole and out the other. He's going to be fine. Just let him sleep. If he wakes up, give him a little whiff."

I assumed it was chloroform, or some such thing. I didn't remember anything after that until I woke for good. Leon was sitting in a chair next to the bed.

"Manon," I said.

He couldn't look at me. I had known Leon since I was 17, and he couldn't look at me.

"Tell me," I said.

"We don't know."

"What do you mean, you don't know?"

"I'm telling you, we don't know."

"But how is that possible?" I said. I was sitting up by then, sort of. Actually, I was propped up on my left elbow. All the weight would be borne by the left side of my body for a while, I guessed.

"How much do you remember?" Leon said.

"I remember being shot, and I remember hearing Manon scream."

"Okay," he said. "Here's what we know. After you went down, Marcel and I dragged your ass out of there as fast as we could and back to the car. The field was dark again by then — the lights all followed the plane. So we couldn't see anything."

"You mean you couldn't see Manon," I said. "So she probably made it on to the plane, right?"

"We're hoping, but we don't know," Leon said. "The next morning, this morning — it's all running together — we went back to the field. There were two bodies there, the men from *Le Franc-Tireur* who had taken Manon to the site and were holding the two torches on that side. They were in a terrible spot — the search lights were hidden in the trees behind them. They were completely lit up. They never had a chance."

"But you didn't find Manon, right?"

"Right," Leon said.

"So that means she made it on to the plane," I said.

"Maybe," he said. "But what if she was wounded and the Gestapo scooped her up for more questioning? Or what if she escaped on her own and is hiding someplace? Or what if—"

"What if she was wounded and died on the plane," I said. It shocked me how matter-of-factly I spoke the sentence.

"Yeah," Leon said. And then the silence crushed us.

We listened to the BBC that night, and there was no message. We didn't know what we were waiting for — there wasn't a pre-arranged code — but we figured we would know it when we heard it. The group surrounding the radio was intense on the one hand and wasted on the other. My pregnant wife was missing, but I still had hope. The other three huddled along with Leon and I had lost close friends on that field, comrades in the greatest brotherhood in France. When they signed up, they knew that danger and death would always be just through the next door, but that never made it any easier. One of the dead men was the brother of the kid sitting to my right. The kid was borderline catatonic.

We listened to the list of favorite new songs, and the recipe for apple pie, and the various birthday greetings, and the snippet from some Shakespeare play, and all the rest, but none of it seemed to apply to us, or Manon, or an airplane under fire. On that much we agreed.

The next night, the same.

The next night, the same.

I was growing frantic. I wanted to find someone willing to go to Montluc with a bundle of women's clothes, on the hope that they would tell us that Manon was there. But it was impossible to ask the men who were hiding in the same cellar as Leon and I. It was just too dangerous. In truth, it likely was suicide.

When the time came on the fourth night, we gathered again around the radio. I still had hope, but I couldn't tell if anyone else did. Even Leon seemed resigned to... something. He was almost as catatonic as the kid.

He stayed that way through the entire broadcast, through the soft snap the knob made when the radio was switched off.

GET A FREE STORY IN THE ALEX KOVACS THRILLER SERIES

My interest is not just in writing, but in building a community of readers. My plan is to be in contact occasionally with news on upcoming books, blog posts and other special offers.

If you sign up to the mailing list, I will send you a **FREE** copy of "Otto's End," a story in the Alex Kovacs thriller series that explains exactly what happened on his trip to Cologne in November of 1936.

It's easy. **IT'S FREE.** Sign up here: https://dl.bookfunnel.com/kpuyzx4un8

ENJOY THIS BOOK? YOU CAN REALLY HELP ME OUT.

The truth is that, as a new author, it is hard to get readers' attention. But if you have read this far, I have yours – and I could use a favor.

Reviews from people who liked this book go a long way toward convincing future readers of its worth. It won't take five minutes of your time, but it would mean a lot to me. Long or short, it doesn't matter.

Thanks!

If you enjoyed this book, please check out my other work. Here's the web address of my Amazon author page:

https://www.amazon.com/author/richardwake

Thanks!

ABOUT THE AUTHOR

Richard Wake is the author of the Alex Kovacs thriller series. His website can be found at richardwake.com. You can connect with Richard on Facebook or you can send him an email at info@richardwake.com.

Made in the USA
San Bernardino, CA
19 May 2019